BROKEN PENCILS

Sharon ~
much appreciation

Victoria Arendt

BROKEN PENCILS

A NOVEL

VICTORIA ARENDT

Published 2020

ISBN 978-1-7346331-7-7 (hardcover) | ISBN 978-1-7346331-4-6 (paperback) | ISBN 978-1-7346331-3-9 (ebook)

Reprinted with permission. Grateful acknowledgement is made to the following for permission to reprint previously published material.

LIFE Magazine: Excerpt from Bedlam by Albert Q. Maisel (LIFE Magazine, 1946), copyright © 1946.
© 1946 The Picture Collection Inc. All rights reserved. Reprinted/Translated from LIFE and published with permission of The Picture Collection Inc. Reproduction in any manner in any language in whole or in part without written permission is prohibited.

Photograph reproduced by permission from Jerry Cooke. © 1946 by Jerry Cooke Archives, Inc.

Cover design by Lance Buckley Designs
Editing by Editegrity

Library of Congress Cataloging-in-Publication Data
Name: Arendt, Victoria
Title: Broken Pencils: a novel | Victoria Arendt p. cm.
Description: Sarasota: Elusive Orao, 2020
Identifiers: LCCN: 2020903365 | ISBN 978-1-7346331-7-7 (hardcover) | ISBN 978-1-7346331-4-6 (paperback) | ISBN 978-1-7346331-3-9 (ebook)

Published by Elusive Orao | www.ElusiveOrao.com | Sarasota, Florida

Printed and bound in the United States of America.

www.BrokenPencilsANovel.com

For my Grandmother,
Mary and The Girls

PROLOGUE

1975

The summer sunshine warmed Ruth's back. A neatly folded towel cushioned her knees and protected her cotton dress from the bright green grass. From time to time she shifted, temporarily relieving the pain in her aging back. A warm breeze swirled around her body, carrying intoxicating floral scents. She plunged a trowel into the ground and sliced the dark, thick soil, watching it separate and crumble. The seedlings Walter bought last week were resting nearby. She reached for one of the containers and brought it to her nose. Her eyes closed as the earthy fragrance filled her senses. The vibrant pink dahlias wouldn't have a scent like her other flowers. She didn't plant them for fragrance. Pinching the bottom of the plastic container, she worked the compacted dirt loose. With each twist, the crackling plastic harmonized with the already peaceful day.

Traffic hummed in the distance, a reminder of the nearby industrial Glass City, but her street was quiet. Occasionally, the peaceful day was interrupted by the crunching of gravel beneath the weight of a vehicle on her road. But moments like that were few. Lunchtime was near and hunger fluttered through her stomach. She thought about the contents in her refrigerator. Walter would be hungry too. After forty-two years together, she was sure of that.

His workshop was steps away from her garden. She could hear clinking and tapping on metal and wood; he was working on projects he would never finish. He had more odds and ends in his workshop than she had in her sewing room. Things, he said, he would use some day. Walter's garage was no longer a garage. Outdated appliances and parts were haphazardly arranged, one on top of another. Despite the open doors, a musky smell of aged lumber, whiskey, and cigars lingered in the workshop. Rusted pieces of iron, their intended use no longer recognizable, leaned against jagged wood scraps piled in a corner. Deteriorated cigar boxes cluttered the workshop, hiding treasures of broken pencils, keys, nails, and an occasional coin or two. Stacks of newspapers sat on top of an old washing machine while a few open pages soaked up oil on the concrete floor. Walter could usually find whatever he was looking for, given enough time. Along the walls were rows of dusty shelves housing tarnished gadgets and stained oil cans, and in the late morning sun through layers of dirt, two mason jars shined, dazzling in blue glass. He said these old gadgets were valuable and would come in handy someday, proudly proving his point by displaying a newer, less reliable appliance made whole again by an old part.

Ruth didn't go into Walter's workshop very often. It was his sanctuary, like the garden was to her. They didn't have much to say anymore. Time stole their conversation. He tinkered in his shop; she pruned her garden. One thing she knew for sure was Walter could fix anything, and with that, she thought about what she would make him for lunch.

She freed a fragile seedling from the plastic when she heard gravel crunching under a moving car. The sound faded as the car drove slowly down the road. Carefully, she placed the seedling in a small divot and pushed cool, loose, dirt around it's waxy roots.

The sound of the crunching gravel became loud again. In a moment, the engine turned off. A car door squeaked open, then closed. She heard footsteps approaching.

"Uh, excuse me," a man's voice called to her.

She pushed herself upward, relieving the ache in her back.

"Are you Mrs. Janikowski? Mrs. Ruth Janikowski?" he asked.

She turned and faced the approaching stranger. He was tall and thin and hobbling toward her. His face looked aged, but his youthful hair gave her the impression he was in his forties.

"Yes, I am," she said. "Can I help you with something?"

He stared at her, then a broad smile crossed his face. He opened his mouth to speak but nothing came out.

A fragrant breeze fluttered her hair, waving white strands against her forehead. She brought her wrist to her face, wiping the hair from her skin. "Can I help you with something?" she repeated.

His face was beaming, his eyes surrounded by wrinkles. He struggled to say something yet remained silent. She no longer heard the distance traffic or felt the breeze through her hair. The ache of her back disappeared as she waited. Each second that passed seemed like an eternity, yet she remained captured by his face.

"Mrs. Janikowski," he finally said. "You saved my life!"

PART I

1932–1933

*It was still quite light out of doors, but inside with the curtains drawn
and the smouldering fire sending out a dim, uncertain glow,
the room was full of deep shadows.*
— KATE CHOPIN

1

EXPOSED MOTOR

Walter inched his way out from underneath his buddy's Model T. The dirt driveway scratched at his back, bunching his T-shirt between his suspenders.

"Stella wants you to come to dinner," Leonard said, "this Saturday night."

His buddy's voice was lighthearted and spirited and hankering for a yes. Walter stood up. He yanked at the back of his shirt and tucked it into his trousers. He didn't look at his buddy but instead opened the accordion hood of the Tin Lizzie.

"She wants you to meet her friend," Leonard continued.

Walter inspected the exposed motor. The years had been good to the engine. He took a closer look. Lifting his head from the compartment he said, "I need a spark plug wrench." He leaned against the car frame, the steel felt warm against his back and fresh air filled his lungs.

His buddy searched through the tool box, steps away from the house. Walter thought of the day he helped Leonard and Stella move in. They didn't have much to move, but Stella made sure he was paid with a hot meal and left with a full stomach that night.

"Here ya go," his buddy said, holding up the wrench.

Walter caught the tool midair and rotated back to the motor. His hands moved around the engine, a twist here and a turn there. "This doll's ready to start," he said. He headed to the front of the Model T. The headlamps seemed to be staring at him and waiting. Wiping the grease from his hands, he pulled the choke. He gripped the crank handle and swung his arm in a semicircle, priming the engine. He waited for Leonard to reach into the car and adjust the throttle and spark lever. A moment later, his buddy gave him the thumbs up.

Planting his feet squarely in front of the Ford, he pulled at his suspenders and prepared for a fight, he gripped the crank with his left hand, clenched the bumper with his right. His feet swiveled deeper down into the dirt as he took a deep breath. He lurched forward forcefully, rotating the crank. The engine sputtered to life.

Leonard adjusted the throttle, slowly smoothing the engine from a rattle to a hum.

"She's purrin' now," Walter said.

His buddy flashed a toothy grin. "Ready for a snort?" he asked.

Walter nodded as the engine sputtered off. He grabbed a dirty handkerchief from his pocket and followed his buddy to the side of the car. His mouth watered as he watched Leonard pull out a bottle from the backseat.

"So, whadda ya say, ole buddy?" Leonard asked. "How's about this Saturday night? Right here."

Stella was a dish, he knew that, but he wasn't so sure her friend would be. "I dunno," he said.

His buddy yanked the cork out with his teeth and spit it into his hand. The running board served as their bar and two shot glasses filled with golden spirits.

"Here's to being dizzy with a dame," his buddy said.

"I dunno 'bout that," he replied, but clinked his glass anyway. He tossed the whiskey to the back of his throat. It burned on its way down, causing a guttural reaction.

The thump of Leonard's hand landing squarely on his back pushed him forward with a jolt. "After all," his buddy said, "You're not getting any younger."

"Yeah, but the dames can't resist—" Walter stopped midsentence at the sound of the screen door. He saw Stella appear on the front porch. Her blonde wavy hair was bouncing under a floppy hat topped by a fluffy white feather.

"Hi, Walter," she called out. Her voice sounded sweet and smoky, just like bourbon.

"Hi ya, Stella," he said. He wished his words sounded as smooth.

She walked down the porch steps, her long legs prancing under a green dress.

He shoved the dirty handkerchief into his pocket and straightened his trousers.

"Did Leonard tell you about dinner?" she asked. "This Saturday night at our house."

"We were just talkin' 'bout that," Leonard said.

"Oh good. Then it's set," she said. "We'll see you at seven." She pointed directly at Walter and added, "Don't be late."

He felt a warm wave rolling from his throat to his face as he watched her walk down the sidewalk.

"Are you going to your mother's?" Leonard called after her.

Her hand waved in the air, her stride not missing a beat.

"I guess we'll see you this Saturday night," Leonard confirmed.

2

LIKE A PAINTING

Walter dabbed his handkerchief on his brow. Stella said he would like her friend, but he wasn't sure. Sure, he was lonely and wouldn't mind the company, but he never found a skirt that could hold his interest. The dames he dated were either too talkative, too shy, or just too ugly. If Stella's friend was any of those, which he was pretty sure she was, he would eat his supper, say he had to help his brother, and leave. Of course, he would say it all rather politely. Besides, he liked being a self-proclaimed wolf in sheep's clothing.

The August evening was hot and humid. The walk to Leonard and Stella's house was a few blocks from his parents. Glancing down each driveway, he counted the number of houses he had worked on and neighbors' cars he had fixed. He was familiar with almost everyone in the Polish neighborhood, so it surprised him when Stella said her friend lived nearby. She must live in the opposite direction.

A couple of elderly Polish ladies sitting on a front porch waved to him. He nodded back. He knew they were wondering where he was going. The old busy bodies knew everything about everybody. He chuckled to himself, thinking of what they were talking about.

His stomach growled, just in time. He had arrived. Leaping up the porch steps, he eyed the new floorboards he and Leonard replaced earlier that summer. But in a moment the atmosphere changed. He stood before the door, surprised at the butterflies in his stomach. Slicking his palm over the side of his hair, he took a deep breath. The sound of voices and laughter echoed from inside. He adjusted his tie, pushing it to his neck, then he opened the screen door and knocked his arrival.

"Walter!" His buddy greeted him at the door.

A few steps inside and the delicious aroma of Stella's cooking circled his nose. His stomach growled again. Leonard started chatting, about his jalopy, or the porch floor, or the Detroit Tigers. He wasn't sure. He was peering into the room beyond. A large, arched entryway led into a candlelit dining room. Stella and her friend were setting the table and giggling. Stella's friend had her back to Walter. He watched her delicate hands place each piece of silverware next to the plates. A pretty belt cinched her slim figure.

So far so good.

Stella's friend paused to straighten a napkin. The entryway framed her like a painting in a museum. Slowly, she moved to the other side of the table, lifting her head. She was smiling and laughing at something Stella had said.

Walter felt his mouth drop open. Leonard's hand landed on his back and it was nudging him through the living room. But his feet wouldn't allow him to step any further. Stella and her friend looked up.

"Walter, this is Ruth. Ruth, this is Walter."

Leonard's words echoed from another world.

He stared at her. Her elegant brown finger waves and

inky penciled brows framed her waltzing chestnut eyes. And her lips. They were ruby. Smiling. At him.

"Nice to meet you, Walter," she said.

He knew his mouth was open but no words came out.

3

SHAKING A WOMAN'S HAND

Ruth's house was several blocks from Walter's, in the opposite direction of Leonard and Stella's. She had gone to the other school. He found that out last Saturday night. She was twenty. Only a three year age difference. Still, he had a lot of questions. *What is her favorite color? Does she have any brothers or sisters? What kind of hobbies does she like?* The questions were written on a folded note in his pocket. Questions and jokes. Just in case. He rubbed the paper, caressing the worn creases between his fingers. The walk seemed long, but he tipped his fedora to everyone and added a polite, "Good evenin'."

Would she be okay with a long walk? He felt his heart flutter. He didn't have a car or much money, but he was one of the lucky ones with a job. That was on his paper too. He wiggled his tie closer to his throat, chuckling at the thought of his brother saying he looked spiffy, trying to impress in his glad rags. He passed another block. A cool summer breeze swirled in the air bringing a whiff of lavender to his nose.

An Irving Berlin melody was stuck in his head. It was the same tune he had been whistling all day. His stride widened. Her house was getting closer. His whistling became louder.

He rubbed the velvety smooth paper in his pocket. He rounded the corner to her parent's block and his pace slowed. The houses on her street seemed well kept, as if no one had lost their job. No peeling paint or weedy yards. And no junk on the front porches. He was walking in front of the first house of the block. Four bold numbers hung on the porch wall: 1159. Her house was steps away. His pulse quickened.

He grabbed his handkerchief and worked it between his clammy hands. A bead of sweat rolled down his face as he read 1155 on the next house. He passed 1151, then 1147. He looked back at the street behind him and almost turned around but didn't. He wiped his face again. Adrenaline shot through his veins as he spotted 1143. Her house.

A two-story beaut'. Thick wooden columns supported a triangular roof that hovered over a sizable house. He approached the porch steps. They looked freshly painted and perfect. He stepped gingerly on each stair, the sunset reflecting on his shiny shoes. The tension in his stomach felt like stinging bees as he stood before the front door. He wanted desperately to rub the soft paper, but instead he knocked on the door.

A pot of red geraniums and a wooden swing hung at the end of the porch. A vision of Ruth flashed through his mind, making the bees sting hard. His wrist dabbed at his forehead. The house numbers stared at him, each metal number secured by two tiny nails. He touched the curve of number three.

The sound of footsteps, inside the house, were getting louder.

He rolled his shoulders back and cleared his throat.

The door opened and a gray-haired man was standing inside—tall and distinguished, he was impeccably dressed. His light blue eyes were piercing, framed in wire glasses that reflected Walter's face.

"You must be Mr. Walter Janikowski," the man said.

Mister. Walter almost turned around, looking for his father.

"Yes," his voice cracked. "I'm here to see Ruth."

"I'm Ollie Urbaniak, Ruth's father," he said.

His handshake was firm and Walter gripped back.

"Please come in," he said.

Walter stepped into the stuffy room. A smell of perfume and bleach bit at his nose. He removed his hat but remained by the entrance, studying the dark living space. The glassy eyes of a stuffed squirrel seemed to be staring at him, watching his every move.

"Can I take your hat?" Ruth's father asked.

He nodded, admiring a carved rosewood bench next to the door.

"My wife got that from one of her customers."

Walter didn't mean to let out a whistle, but out it came.

"Would you like a snort?" her father asked.

Leonard had warned him not to drink too much of the giggle juice and to keep his wits about him, especially around her parents, but Walter didn't want to be impolite. They clinked shot glasses and soon the living room began to fill. Ruth and two older women came in together, and a handful of kids hid behind stair rungs, watching and grinning.

Walter was surprised at Ruth's mother's handshake, strong like a man's. He was not used to shaking a woman's hand.

"Do you have a job?" she asked as their eyes met.

He was prepared for questions like that, ready to impress with his quick wit. But when he opened his mouth to answer, she fired another question, and another, and another, faster than a Tommy Gun.

"What does your father do?"

"Where are your parents from?"

"What grade did you complete?"

Her powerful voice ricocheted off every angle. He felt beads of sweat form on his brow and he itched to touch the folded paper. When he tried to answer, there she was again, with another question. Ruth jumped in, skillfully maneuvering the conversation to a congenial tone and soon, they were out the door.

The evening air felt cool against his damp skin but he could feel perspiration trickling down his temple. He looked at Ruth. The porch light bounced off her chestnut eyes. A tiny image of himself appeared in her pupil. She smiled, a soft lovely smile. Her gentle, cool fingers whisked a droplet of sweat from his skin. The bees turned into butterflies.

4

NAMESAKE

During their courtship, Walter took Ruth to the movie theater a few times but only once after they wed. The house they moved into was directly across the street from the theater and as the due date of their first child neared, she seemed to be searching for a distraction. He watched as she paced the living room, looking at the theater across the street. She said her mother warned her to stay out of sight, but he knew his wife had a mind of her own. Each week, the theater banners were replaced with new ones broadcasting the latest feature. And each week, he found reviews and tidbits about spy films and actors on scraps of paper in his lunch pail or on top of his workshop bench.

"Okay, okay," he said. *Duck Soup* was playing and although he was sure she wasn't interested in the Four Marx Brothers, he understood she just wanted to get out of the house.

As the starting time of the movie approached, she put on one of his overcoats, telling him she was concealing her round belly. He told her she looked nice, but she really looked like a pretty hobo. He saw her staring out the window, telling him she wanted to wait for the ticket line to dwindle before they went out. "Okay," she said. "The last couple has gone inside. Are you ready?"

He was tying his oxfords when she yanked his coat from the rack. Her feet were tapping clumsily in a pair of large overboots. It reminded him of a clown.

"I'm ready. I'm ready," he said, standing up.

He took the coat from her, slid one arm inside, then the other.

"Don't forget the pencil behind your ear," she said.

He had been using the pencil earlier to sketch diagrams of toys and blocks he planned on making for the baby. He was sure it was going to be a boy, and they had already decided to name him Walter Junior, his namesake. He was proud of that name. He planned on teaching him how to build things and fix things. He was going to be a smart boy, and while Walter would rather be making toys than going to the movies, at least he was going to see Groucho Marx.

She leaned into him and plucked the pencil out from behind his ear. She tried to put his hat on, too, but she couldn't reach the top of his head.

Flipping up his coat collar, he declared he was ready to go.

A freezing draft swirled into the room with the opening of the front door. His cheeks were stung by the icy air as they stepped outside. Shimmering in the moonlight, the porch was an iridescent blue. He had shoveled the sidewalk earlier, and now shadowy lines glistened against snow-covered yards. Walter watched Ruth grab the handrail, as she moved, she placed each foot at a strange angle on the steps.

"It's colder than I thought," she said.

The street lamps gave the night air a quiet hum. Across the road, the marquee created a festive garland of light that reflected off the hoods and roofs of the tightly parked cars.

As they crossed the street, they stepped through crunchy slush lines left behind by the day's plow. Ruth shimmied between two cars, grabbing a Cadillac headlamp and the back of a Buick luggage box to steady her footing. She looked like a perpendicular zeppelin slipping through a narrow gorge. The closer they got to the building, the louder the theater lights buzzed. A warm glow flooded the sidewalk as it changed its color from purple to gray.

Walter stepped up to the box office and peered through the glass. The ticket agent was plucking quarters from a pile, building stacks of coins as his lips silently counted. Walter positioned his face in front of a small round opening and leaned in. "Two tickets please," he said, watching the steam rise out of his mouth.

"That'll be fifty cent, Sir," the agent said.

Walter plunged his hand in his pants pocket and pulled out two coins. The quarters clinked as he dropped them into the empty scoop under the glass.

The agent's skinny fingers pulled at the coins, replacing them with tickets. "Go right in," he said.

Ruth was smiling as he escorted her to the entrance. He tugged at the front door, but it didn't open. He tugged again and it still didn't open. Ruth's expression turned into one of panic. He pulled the door one more time, then pushed, and it opened. He heard her chuckle, and it made him chuckle too.

The entrance was empty, but the space was filled with spirit and life. The aroma of popcorn and bootleg whiskey made his mouth water. He removed his steamy glasses, wiping them against his coat. Bright yellow posters with big red letters covered the walls with faces of the Four Marx Brothers in *Duck Soup*. He looked at the concession counter but it was empty.

The coat check man took their coats and replaced them with a ticket, then they walked down a skinny walkway lined with red ropes and golden poles leading to two closed doors. Walter carefully pushed and pulled until one of the doors opened. The theater was dark. They paused at the entrance and as linked rows of seats came into focus, they saw the room was full. Hushed voices and quiet laughter bounced from the elevated ceiling. A gradually sloping aisle led to a large, blank movie screen. Eyeing a few empty seats in the front row, he began to walk down the aisle, but felt Ruth's hand on his arm, stopping him in his tracks. She pointed to two seats in the very back.

"Excuse us," she said to a couple in the row. "Are those two taken?"

They shook their heads.

Ruth told him to go in first. He squeezed past the couple, shuffling to a seat. The lights started to flicker. The room turned dark. The whirl of the projector started and a silent liveliness swept over the audience. *Clang, Clang, Clang!* The movie began with a bang. He laughed and slapped his knee at Groucho Marx's antics throughout the show. And, soon enough, the movie was almost over.

Ruth nudged his arm. "Let's leave," she whispered.

He glanced at her. "Leave?"

"I want to sneak out before everybody else," she said.

He looked at the screen. Groucho was at it again. He laughed and laughed until she tugged at his arm. He slowly stood up and inched his way out of the aisle.

PART II

1934–1937

Whoso loves
Believes the impossible.
— ELIZABETH BARRETT BROWNING

5

TIRE TRACKS

Walter watched Ruth as she pondered their living room.

"Maybe a little closer that way," she said, pointing toward the window.

He pushed a red velvet chair closer to the front of the living room. Despite the sparse mix of furniture from his relatives and hers, he liked how she made the room cozy and inviting. The red velvet chair was the latest addition, an inheritance from Ruth's spinster Aunt Bessie. Ruth said she used to sit in the chair as a little girl, tracing the vertical peacock tufts with her fingers. She told him her aunt had said she looked like a princess sitting in the chair. He thought the chair's spindly maple legs resembled the thin calves of Aunt Bessie; both had to support plump bodies. He heard her sigh. She still wasn't satisfied, he could tell.

"No, he might feel a draft," she said.

This wasn't the first inherited piece of furniture he moved around the room, and he knew it wouldn't be the last. He placed his hands on the back of the chair. The fabric was in good condition for its age, smooth and soft, no matter which way he rubbed it.

"Maybe a little the other way," she said. Her hand waved in the opposite direction.

He pulled the chair across the brown area rug, the spindly legs forging tire tracks along the way. He folded his arms and rested on the back of the chair, waiting for the next set of instructions.

She was eyeing the room again. He watched her walk from one side to the other.

"Maybe we should move it closer to the bedroom," she said.

He scooted the chair across the room, the ruts in the carpet becoming busier.

"No. That's too much," she said.

He scooted it back.

She sighed.

It was a quiet sigh, but he heard it.

"I'm not sure," she said. "What do you think?"

"Whatever you think," he answered. "You're gonna be the one sitting here with him."

A quick short breath escaped her, this one wasn't so quiet. "I just want it to be right," she said. "I want him to be able to see outside and watch the theater across the street. I want everything perfect for him."

"He's a baby, Ruth," he said.

"I know, I know. I just want him to be happy."

He looked around the room. His hands dropped from the chair. He took a few steps backward. "This is pretty good," he said. "And you can feed him while lookin' outside. And the radiator's right here for winter. I'll put the footstool under the chair." He slid the matching footstool underneath the puffy seat.

"Perfect!" she replied.

He was sure the chair was back in its original position.

6

YELLOW CANDLES

Ruth leaned forward and studied her face in the mirror. After months of stuffy indoor confinement, her and Junior's hibernation was over. She picked up her shiny gold lipstick tube. It felt cold and smooth. Heeding the unwanted advice of her mother, she waited almost a year before returning to the ladies' church brunch. She tugged at the lipstick cap, popping it free. Each twist of her hand revealed a dark shade of ruby growing taller and taller. She stained her lips and pressed them together. Walter's white handkerchief would soon have a red kiss.

She glanced at Junior. His crib was in the corner of her and Walter's bedroom. It was a gift from his parents, like the secondhand oak dresser next to it. She recalled spending a month polishing the scuffs and scratches, wanting to vindicate the shabby pieces sitting next to the flawless mahogany bed donated by her mother.

A few moments later, she was outside with Junior, pushing his baby buggy. The sunshine cut through the last of the winter chill, releasing spring air into the morning. Sprouts of vibrant green grass and pink tulips brightened the brisk walk to the church. She hoped Mrs. Kowalski would be the first to meet Junior. Ruth knew the woman loved her like Edna, her own daughter. Ruth glanced at her knuckle. The hopscotch scar was still there, a reminder of her best friend. It felt like just yesterday they met on Ruth's first day of school. The teacher showed her a seat next to a dainty blonde girl. Edna was her name. They soon became friends through whispers of boys and glances from the nuns. As each school year passed, they became inseparable—until their sophomore year, when Edna met Norman. No one was surprised they married right after graduation. Norman took a job in Wisconsin and they were gone.

Caught in her memories, Ruth and the buggy stumbled over a sidewalk tree root. She gripped the handle and steadied the wobbling wheels. A faint whimper drifted from Junior. She looked inside the buggy. Sunlight beamed on his face, and his eyelashes fluttered like a humming bird's wings. She adjusted the hood and continued walking. The church was on the next block. It stood majestic, protecting one corner of the neighborhood. Graceful, soaring windows defined by dark brick brought her eye to a steeply pitched gable roofline. Above a set of elegant white doors was a large stained glass window. Above that was a circular rose mullion, a belfry, a lantern, and finally, a thin, light blue spire. Along the base of the church, several empty baby buggies were parked like miniature cars. She maneuvered Junior's buggy to the end of the row, parking it a safe distance from the others. Unhitching a bag from Walter's homemade clip, she stuffed extra diapers into the sack and slung it over her shoulder. Junior's eyes slowly opened as she lifted him up.

She turned and faced the church. Looking up, she marveled at the tall, pointed steeple piercing the bright blue sky. Spring air filled her lungs. For a moment, the steeple seemed to sway, causing her quickly to refocus her attention on the cement stairs before her. She hugged Junior closer to her body and carefully stepped on each wide step until they reached the top. The entrance doors were closed. She tugged at one of the doors. It was heavy but opened with a whoosh. The church foyer was quiet and deserted. The door closed slowly behind her and the room darkened. A dangling chandelier tinkled in the drafty space. In the corner stood a miniature table crowded with tiny yellow candles, whose flames flickered against ruby red glass and cast ominous shadows on the walls. A thin trail of smoke floated from a pewter ashtray, unleashing the smell of sulfur.

She quietly moved deeper into the building. The small, dark vestibule gave way to a massive, empty cathedral illuminated by colorful prisms of light shimmering through stained glass windows. Colossal arches soared from the peaked windows outlining an ornate ceiling bordered in damask blood red wallpaper. Biblical baroque paintings hung between each window depicting the Stations of the Cross.

Dipping her fingertips in a marble basin of holy water, she made the sign of the cross and touched the back of Junior's head. She paused for a moment. Repetitive rows of wooden pews flanked the center aisle, leading to an ostentatious gold altar adorned with solemn white statues forever in worship. Then she turned around. Heavy purple curtains covered shelves and cabinets hidden along the back wall, concealing a passageway to the basement. She opened the door. A dimly lit narrow stairwell appeared bottomless. The church was over fifty years old, but the plaster of the dingy walls seemed unfinished and hurriedly slapped on. Taking a deep breath, she grabbed the railing and began her gradual descent. She adjusted her grip only after angling each foot on the narrow steps, securing her footing. Slowly, she moved deeper into the cavern. Junior wiggled. She froze midstep and tightened her hand on the rail. She whispered his name. He burrowed back in his blanket before she continued the descent. At the bottom of the stairs, muffled voices resonated through the closed door. She reached for the handle. The cold metal stung her skin as she pulled the door open.

Tubes of fluorescent bulbs hung from the ceiling, flooding the church basement with an abundance of bright light. The clamorous sounds of chitchat and laughter ricocheted in every direction. She kept Junior close to her body and despite their noisy surroundings, his head rested peacefully on her shoulder. Shifting his weight, she cautiously slid her jacket sleeve off one arm, letting the garment dangle, empty spirited. A woman nearby helped her remove the coat and hung it on a rolling rack. Ruth scanned the room. Ladies arrayed in colorful tea dresses made from crepe, chiffon, and silk formed tight circles. Rows of long, rectangular tables were covered in white linen, glistening china and silverware, with shiny candelabras dotting the centers. Off to the side, a group of women sat at the end of a table, huddling and whispering, only interrupted by their own random bursts of laughter.

She could not see Mrs. Kowalski but her eyes landed on two small boys holding paper airplanes. They dashed through one of the tight circles causing it to temporality split. She caught a glimpse of her target at the back of the room. She waved. "Mrs. Kowalski!" she called, her words were lost in the sea of voices.

Making her way through the crowd, she heard her name.

"Ruthie, over here!" Gladys was waving to her from a circle of childhood classmates.

"Hi Gladys!" she responded. "I'll be right back." Gladys smiled and nodded.

A mixture of aromas filled the room, bringing whiffs of bacon, coffee, and perfume to her nose. She was heading toward the back of the room, but lost sight of Mrs. Kowalski. A robust woman wearing a loosely wrapped apron passed in front of her, stopping at a nearby table to fill empty coffee cups. Ruth bobbed and weaved through the clumps of women, threading her way toward the back of the room. Her hand covered Junior's head from arms spearing from the talkative groups.

She spotted Mrs. Kowalski again. "Mrs. Kowalski!" she called. Her words reached the target.

"Ruthie!" Mrs. Kowalski's booming voice reverberated as she rushed over.

Ruth and Junior were engulfed in the woman's large frame.

"How are you?" Mrs. Kowalski began. A tendril of wiry gray hair had wiggled loose from her bun. Her pudgy fingers grasped the strand and tucked it around her ear.

"I'm glad you're here," they said in unison.

"Is Josephine here too?" Mrs. Kowalski asked. Her round spectacles rested on top of her cheeks, moving with each word about Ruth's mother.

Ruth shook her head. She saw Mrs. Kowalski's eyes focus on the back of Junior's blanketed body.

"And is this the new bundle of joy?" Mrs. Kowalski asked.

Ruth snuggled Junior to her chest. "Yes," she said. "I wanted you to be the first to meet Walter Junior. We call him Junior." She lowered Junior from her shoulder. He was about to meet the world.

"And let's meet this handsome little—" Mrs. Kowalski's words stopped.

"He's cute as a button, isn't he?"

"He's … um … yes, of course, cute as a button."

Ruth beamed and gave Junior a squeeze. "He's a little different," she said. "But I just knew you'd love him. I'm gonna introduce him to Gladys and the girls."

She saw Mrs. Kowalski's eyes darting back and forth around the room before they landed back on her.

"Wait," Mrs. Kowalski whispered.

Ruth pulled herself from Mrs. Kowalski's grasp and headed for Gladys's circle.

"Oh, Ruth, let's meet him properly," Gladys said. "Have a seat."

One of the women dragged a chair from a nearby table. Excitement buzzed from her group of friends as she shifted Junior to her lap. The room turned warmer as the ladies gathered tightly around her chair, their pretty shoes pointing at her son. She kissed his forehead, wanting him to open his eyes.

The cooing and chirping suddenly stopped. The pretty shoes disappeared.

A couple of boys ran up to her chair. They pulled at Junior's blanket, exposing more of his body.

The once well-formed circles were now rows of women, lining the edges of the room. The clanking of silverware and laughter fell to murmurs and whispers.

"Look," pointed one of the boys. "It's baby Frankenstein!"

"No," cried another, "it's the Hunchback of Notre Dame!"

"He's a little different," Ruth said, "that's all." She looked up at her friends, their faces no longer recognizable.

7

SHIELDING

U NION STRIKES!
The bold black letters covered the front page
of the newspaper that shielded Walter from Ruth.
She watched his knuckles turn white as he gripped the
pages, curling the top corners.

"Those auto strikes," he said. "They're getting vicious
again."

She watched as he gave the paper a quick flick, standing
the pages back to attention. "You're not gonna go out and
protest again. Are you?" She hoped her voice didn't sound
alarmed but his breakfast plate wobbled when she set it
down.

Junior squealed and kicked the tray of his high chair.
She stepped close to her son and tugged at his seatbelt, the
one Walter added a few days ago.

"I hope your mother appreciates that pie," Walter said,
slapping the newspaper closed.

She looked at Walter. He was nodding to the rolling pin
and apples on the counter.

"It's a small pie," she answered.

"Yeah, but we're down to our last two bits until payday," he said.

She grabbed the coffee pot. A nutty aroma snaked its way to her nose. "I know," she said, "but this is only the second time my mother has come to visit him." She didn't want to think about the past eight months and how she tried to convince her mother to spend time with her own grandson. Even though she wasn't looking at Walter, she knew he was shaking his head.

"How long is she gonna to stay?" he asked.

"I don't know. Hopefully awhile, so she gets to know him."

"He's better off not knowing her," he said through a mouthful of eggs.

"She's not that bad."

"If you say so," he added. He stood up and put on his coat.

"Wish me luck," she said.

"You're gonna need it."

She heard the backdoor shut as Walter left and quickly brought the breakfast dishes to the sink. The pipes howled as she turned the faucet on and doused a washcloth. Walter's old Model T puttered backward down the driveway, slowly passing the kitchen window. Glancing at the wall clock, she planned for an early arrival.

8

PEOPLE TALK

A distinguishable knock reverberated throughout the house. Thirty minutes early. Ruth turned over a tiny kitchen timer, allowing the sand to start pouring into the bottom of the hourglass. A quick tug to her apron bow, and the material went slack.

The bold knock sounded again.

Lifting the apron over her head, the strap pulled at her brown hair.

"Coming!" she said. She tossed the apron on the counter and rushed into the spotless living room. Everything, including the empty baby basket, was in its place. Earlier, she placed Junior in his crib. He was cranky and tired, and she wanted him to be rested for the visit.

Another sharp knock.

Glancing at the hall mirror, she smoothed her hair then opened the door.

Her mother's towering physique filled the doorframe. Despite the sunny autumn day, her mother wore a wool coat and brown hat, like Eleanor Roosevelt ready to deliver a speech.

"Hello, Mother," Ruth said. "Nice to see you."

"Hello, Ruth." The deep, throaty words had a distinguishable Polish accent.

Her mother stepped into the living room, pinching and tugging at her gloves and loosening each finger.

"Can I take your coat?" Ruth asked.

Silky white gloves dropped into her open palms without a word. Her mother turned and extended her arms backward to Ruth.

"Your dress looks lovely," Ruth said, placing the coat on a rack.

Her mother's head lowered. Her hands moved down the front of her gray plaid dress. "Yes," she said. "This is from The Lion Store."

Ruth frowned at the thought of her father struggling with the striking workers. She smoothed the front of her own dress.

"I see you're wearing that old thing again," her mother said.

Ruth touched the fraying fabric close to her neck.

"It seems Walter can't afford anything new," her mother continued. "I'll see if one of my customers has a dress they can give you."

Ruth looked at the front door. It was closed but she could easily open it and push her out. "Have a seat," she said instead.

She watched her mother examine the room, glancing at everything, then focusing on the red velvet chair. Irritation pulled at Ruth's neck as she remembered the day the chair was delivered, her mother telling Walter they needed all the donations they could get.

Her mother marched to the chair, the floor boards thumping beneath each step.

"How was the walk over here?" Ruth asked, taking a seat on the edge of the sofa.

A forceful breath released from her mother as she

plopped into the velvet seat, the spindly chair legs moving over the rug.

"Sit up straight, Ruth," came the reply.

She rolled her shoulders back and lifted her head. "I've made an apple pie," she said. "Just for you. I'm using the new recipe we talked about. Remember?"

"Mm hmm," she replied. "Did I tell you about Margaret's pies? They are so light and flaky and break apart."

Ruth forced a smile as she watched her mother's fingers drumming the chair arms, eyeing everything in the room.

"The weather's nice today," Ruth said. "Isn't it?"

Her mother remained rigid and straight. "Yes," she replied. "It is."

Ruth followed her gaze to Junior's empty basket. "Walter made that last week. It's perfect for Junior," she said.

Her mother's fingers sped up their drumming.

"It's pretty good, isn't it?" Ruth asked.

"What's good?"

"The basket." She watched her mother look at the basket again.

"Yes," she said. "I suppose so."

"Walter is very talented. He can make useful things from junk. Why, just the other day, he added a belt to Junior's highchair to keep him from slipping out. He made it from an old strap of something," she said. "Isn't that wonderful?"

Her mother didn't answer but kept looking around the room.

Ruth heard Junior's cry. "Oh good! He's awake," she said. "I'll be right back."

The bedroom was warm. Junior was crying and wiggling in his crib and his blanket was balled up at the end of the mattress. She picked him up and cuddled him to her shoulder. His skin was damp. She buried her nose in his hair, smelling the sweet scent. As she carried him to the door, she caught her mother's gaze darting away from the bedroom and back into the living room.

Junior's cries turned to whimpers with each bounce and step. "Okay," she whispered in his ear, "let's play with Busia." She faced her mother. "Would you like to hold him?"

"Has the boy rolled over yet?" she asked.

"No, not yet," Ruth answered. "But he will soon."

"He should have already rolled over by now. Dr. Edwards said——"

"Oh, Mother, he's fine. He's learning every day." She pulled Junior closer to her chest and rubbed his back.

"He looks funny," her mother said. "People talk."

Ruth sat on the sofa and held Junior in the air, his legs wiggled and dangled above her knees. "I think he's cute as a bug's ear," she said. "Look at the bubbles between his lips. Isn't he cute?" She looked over at her mother.

Her glasses were at the end of her nose, her chin tilted upward. "If you say so," she said.

"People need to get to know him. You need to get to know him. He's a good boy, Mother." She arranged Junior on her lap facing his grandmother.

"How's that husband of yours?" her mother asked. "He hasn't lost his job yet, has he?"

"Mother, Walter's working very hard. We're just fine. Let's have a nice visit."

The tapping started again, making the room seem almost empty.

"I'm going to check the pie," Ruth said. She quickly rose from the sofa and placed Junior in her mother's lap then exited the room.

The aroma of coffee and cinnamon became stronger as she stepped into the kitchen. The top of the hour glass was empty and the bottom was a pyramid of sand. She slipped a potholder on and opened the oven. A steamy fragrance of apple billowed out and the crust was golden brown. She took the pie out.

Quietly she moved to the living room doorway. Junior was blinking at his grandmother. She knew his long, fluttery eyelashes could melt even the hardest of hearts, but her mother kept him at the end of her knees.

Back in the kitchen, Ruth arranged coffee cups on a tray as Junior began to cry. She looked into the living room again. "Just rock him in your arms," she said. "That usually makes him stop." Junior was still at the end of her mother's lap. His face began to scrunch up. His fleshy tongue poked out and percolated a gurgle. A cough spiked the air and a glistening piece of spit hurling straight at her mother's face.

The sound of disgust coming from her mother made her skin crawl. She ran back into the living room and grabbed Junior. "Let me take him," she said. "The pie is cooling, and I've got fresh coffee, too."

Her mother was smoothing her dress, flicking what seemed to be dirt from her lap.

"How's Father?" Ruth asked.

"Oh, he's always at the factory," she said. "Did you know Margaret and Edward are moving to Detroit? He's gotten a huge promotion."

"Oh. That's good news," she said. "Walter's up for a promotion, too."

Her mother was about to say something but Ruth was quicker. "The pie's ready," she said. She placed Junior in his baby basket, then added, "Keep an eye on him for me." Stepping out of the room, she heard her mother whisper to Junior.

"You know you embarrass the family."

Ruth stopped. Her back straightened. The eagerness of having her mother visit was replaced by an eagerness for her to leave.

"By the way," her mother's voice was loud, as if Ruth was already back in the kitchen. "I can't stay too long."

Ruth took a deep breath. "Do you want cream and sugar with your coffee?" she asked.

"No, I'm watching my figure."

Ruth returned with the coffee tray and two pieces of pie.

"Just a small taste," her mother said. Ruth watched as her mother sliced into the pie, scooping a large triangular piece onto her fork. She chewed the first bite, then sliced another.

"Well?" Ruth asked.

The chewing continued. Her mother set the fork on the empty plate. "Well," she said, "I must be leaving."

"Do you like my pie?" Ruth asked.

"Oh, yes. It's good. Next time," she said, "use Margaret's recipe. You know how good a baker your sister is."

Her mother stood up and walked to the door.

Ruth followed her and grabbed her coat. "Oh," she said, "Can you watch Junior one evening this weekend? *The Richest Girl in the World* is playing across the street. Gladys said its funny. Miriam Hopkins, Faye Wray pretend to be—"

"Ruth, you know I'm busy," she said. "I have alterations to finish. You know your father doesn't make much, especially with the strike."

She picked up her mother's gloves.

"And you need to have Dr. Edwards look at the boy again. He's—"

"He's just fine," Ruth said.

"He's feeble minded," she said. "Broken. A lunatic asylum is where—"

"No. He's not going in one of those." She slapped the gloves in her mother's palm.

"They will handle him better than you, Ruth. Dr.

Edwards said he will never talk or think or feed himself. Or do anything."

"I feed him and do everything."

"You want to change diapers for the rest of your life? He's gonna get big and strong. Then what?"

"Mother, I can handle him."

"What if you have another baby?" she said. "How are you gonna take care of a baby and a boy that's like a baby? Have you ever thought of that?"

She watched her mother button her coat. The fabric puckered as her gloved fingers pushed the fasteners through each hole.

"He's broken," her mother said. "He will always be broken."

"How can you say that about your own grandson? No. He's fine. And I will do whatever it takes to keep him out of those snake pits. And that's final."

"Well, then ask Dr. Edwards what you did to have a baby like that," her mother said. "You don't want another one like him."

9

FEEBLE MINDED

"When he's done, can you lift him for me?" Ruth looked at Walter. He was at the opposite end of the table from her and Junior. Still dressed in his factory shirt, his rolled sleeves revealed muscular forearms and callused hands. Before supper, she handed him a scrub brush, but she wasn't sure he used it. "I don't need a lot of help," she added. "Just with lifting him. And only now and then. Dr. Edwards doesn't want me to strain." She rubbed the side of her belly thinking about the doctor's words.

Walter was shoveling a piece of meatloaf into his mouth and mumbled a response.

She couldn't understand what he said, but she knew it was an affirmative mumble. Steadying herself against the table, she balanced the weight of her belly over her frame and stood up. Her cotton housedress kept her cool, hanging loosely around her expectant shape. Her canvas slippers hugged her swollen feet as she shuffled to the icebox. "Mother says I need to do better this time around," she said. "And that it's gonna be too hard for me to care for a baby and Junior. But I can do it, I know I can."

Junior's high pitched squeal pierced the air.

She shuffled over to him. His fists swirled and banged down on his tray, flattening mashed potatoes into an unknown map. Grabbing his hands, she rubbed a napkin over his mush-covered fingers. "She keeps saying Junior is an embarrassment and should be put in the insane asylum."

A quick loud breath sounded from Walter.

She looked at him. His hand was paused over his plate, a piece of meatloaf dangling from his fork. The air felt thin, the kitchen sharply still. She inhaled what little air was left and continued. "Dr. Edwards doesn't know if this baby will be okay. I'm worried."

He slowly set his fork down. The lone piece of meatloaf rested on narrow tracks of gravy. His brawny hands moved to the edge of the table, pushing his chair back, scraping it against the floor.

Junior squealed.

"Everything will be fine," he said. His voice sounded tight and controlled. She watched as he turned around and vanished from the room. The workshop screen door squeaked open, then banged shut.

She reached for a tin can filled with coffee. Her fingers concealed an Indian on the bright coffee label as Dr. Edwards' words echoed in her head.

He's permanently feeble minded. An imbecile.

She stuck a butter knife under the coffee lid, twirling the can and loosening the tin disk until it popped off.

He will always have the mind of a two year old.

She brought the can to her nose.

He will always need care.

The coffee beans jingled as she poured them into a wooden grinder. Junior squealed at the sounds. Rotating the grinder arm, she crushed and pulverized the beans.

A mental hygiene institution is the place for people like him.

10

LAVENDER NIGHT

T ugging the backdoor open, Ruth entered the balmy, moonless evening. Golden light beamed through her kitchen window as locusts buzzed in the warm air. Earlier that summer, Walter unearthed sections of bumpy grass, replacing the divots with flat stones that led to a wandering path to his workshop. The stones were still warm from the day, infiltrating her slippers and warming the soles of her feet. She knew Walter didn't like to be disturbed when he was working, but Dr. Edwards told her not to lift Junior, not in her condition.

She stepped further along the path. A lightning bug flittered in front of her face, its orange lantern illuminating a small dot of the night. Her hands floated to the bug but it flew higher into the sky. A breeze of sweet lavender swirled around her, stroking her cheeks with strands of her hair. The closer she stepped toward the workshop, the brighter the path became. Amber light and a faint hum emanated from the small shed. The screen door latch felt cool as she pulled the door open. The familiar squeak announced her presence.

Humming on Walter's work table was a miniature metal

fan. The blades spun a lazy whirl and dirty white ribbons fluttered in the air. A single bulb hung motionless in the center of the room; its pull chain resting against the orb and saturating an area with a circle of light. The smell of cigar smoke and whiskey replaced lavender.

She looked at Walter. He was hunched over his worktable with a stubby cigar hanging from his lips. Swooped over his forehead was a slicked strand of Brylcreem hair, a pencil tucked behind his ear. He appeared to be studying a small gadget in his hand.

Leaning against a splintered shelf, she remained by the door. The coolness from the concrete floor stole the warmth from the stones. Bright red ash flashed from the end of Walter's cigar and dark sweat stains seeped through his work shirt, sticking the material to his body. Turning the metal object from side to side, his brow furrowed. A puff of smoke escaped his lips, meandering to the solitary bulb.

"Can you help me lift Junior from his chair?" she asked.

He set the gadget down and adjusted his glasses. His index finger curled around the short cigar and pulled it from his mouth. Walking past her to the door, he pushed the screen door open and held it open for her. The lavender night filled with cigar smoke. She watched his wide stride carry him over two stones at a time, his work boots pounding with each step. She squinted at the path, her slippers gingerly finding each stone.

The kitchen was warm from the oven heat, the aroma of coffee and garlic saturated the air. She looked at Junior. He was securely belted in his chair, his arms waving above his head, conducting a silent orchestra.

"Stay still," she said. She unbuckled his seatbelt but his legs still kicked and bounced. Walter was standing at his end of the table, his hands clasped to the back of his chair. "You might want to remove the pencil," she said. "Remember how he broke it last night?"

He pulled the pencil from behind his ear and removed his glasses. Adjusting his shirt, she thought he looked like he was preparing for an interview.

"Okay," she said. She took a few steps backward.

Walter didn't move.

"He's not going to bite," she said.

He stepped toward Junior. Junior grunted. His arms and legs kicked and punched the air. She watched as Walter bobbed and weaved, timing his reach toward Junior, finally swooping in and grabbing him. He hoisted him out of his chair, dangling him like a sack of potatoes. Junior's arm swung. Walter's head pitched to the side, missing the small fist.

"Put him on the floor against the cabinets," she said.

Walter place him on the floor.

"It's okay, Junior," she said. She removed the upper chamber from the vacuum coffee maker and set it on its stand. The lower chamber was full of hot, brown liquid. Reaching for two cups, she placed them on their saucers. "Do you want your coffee in here with us?" she asked.

She glanced at Walter. His glasses were back on and the pencil was behind his ear, but he was looking at Junior. "No," he said.

She handed him his coffee. His large fingers wrapped around the saucer, rattling the china.

Junior squealed.

She propped her body against the kitchen counter and watched Walter walk out the backdoor.

Dr. Edwards' words were echoing again.

He's permanently feeble minded.

There's no guarantee your next baby will not be like him.

Ruth wrapped Junior's hands around his baby bottle. "Grab the bottle," she said. She slowly removed her fingers.

The bottle dropped to his lap.

11

HIGHLIGHTED BY THE ABNORMAL

W alter touched the wooden rails. The paint was finally dry. He pulled his cigar from his mouth and placed it in his workshop ashtray. The playpen wasn't heavy but cumbersome as he carried it into the house. He spotted Ruth in the living room, waiting. She had George in her arms and Junior on the floor between her feet. The paint took longer to dry than he thought it would, but she was smiling.

"Set it down right there," she said.

He put it down.

"Will you put the blanket on the bottom?" she asked.

He unfolded the blanket and spread it across the playpen base. The excess fabric bunched at the rails.

"Now, will you put him in it?"

She stepped away from Junior. He wobbled without the support of her legs, almost falling over, but Walter swooped in and placed him inside the playpen. He looked at his son, and the way his suspenders pinched the top of his trousers, the baggy material accentuating his awkwardly folded legs.

"Will you put his can on his lap?" she asked.

Walter picked up the toy he made last weekend. Ruth

said she couldn't get Junior interested in playing with building blocks or wooden cars but he solved the toy crisis with an empty coffee can. The coffee label had bright red and white letters and an Indian surrounded by a halo of yellow. Ruth said she liked the way the Warrior looked, his fierce silhouette had an immortal stare, like Junior did sometimes. Walter had filled the can with a handful of blue marbles, securely pounding the tin lid closed. Each shake and roll triggered rattles, jingling like coins. And it worked. Junior seemed to like the toy.

He watched his wife wiggle into the velvet chair, feeding George his bottle. He recalled the day George was born and how relieved he felt when Dr. Edwards said he was a normal baby boy. Then he looked at Junior. The unusual curvature of his skull was highlighted by the abnormal way his head rested against two rails. The can slowly rolled between his legs. His bony fists clenched and shook with the sounds.

A Model A puttered passed the living room window, sending a brilliant flicker of sunshine across Walter's face. He shielded his eyes and looked down at a glistening snow pile near the driveway, the only snow remaining from last week's snowstorm. Despite the sunny spring sky, the bitter winter temperatures lingered, keeping the pile intact.

He looked across the road to the theater, a stately brick building with a rolling arched roofline. Fastened to its triangular marquee, simple neon letters proclaimed Liberty. In a few hours, rows of tightly parked cars will border the street, and people bundled in coats and hats will wait in line to see *A Family Affair*, starring Lionel Barrymore. Last year, renovations to the theater began and Ruth said her chair was the front row. Each night at supper, she updated him with the latest and laughed at how roadsters and socialites were replaced with work trucks and carpenters.

"I wonder what the theater looks like now," she said.

Walter wondered how she had read his mind.

12

SKINNY PATHWAY

A stream of sunlight meandered through the bedroom window, beaming into a bowl of lavender sachets. A calming mixture of perfume and baby powder weaved its way into Ruth's nose. She inhaled the scent, relieved she finally got George to settle down for a nap. His crib was next to the oak dresser, partially blocking the closet. Junior's crib was wedged in a corner but he was in the living room, sitting in his playpen. She navigated the skinny pathway to Junior's crib and folded the blanket inside. She touched his sheets. They were damp. Pulling them from the small mattress, she bundled them under her arm and stepped around her and Walter's bed. The intricate crochet bedspread was rumpled. She pulled the delicate weave straight, its scalloped edges dusting the dark wooden floor. Her side of the bed was the one closest to Junior and their tiny bedroom seemed to be continually shrinking.

Walter suggested moving the cribs upstairs, unsure why she didn't use the vacant second floor. But she insisted the boys weren't ready. She leaned across the oak dresser toward the window. Gripping the thick curtain cord, she inched the heavy golden drapes closed. She tiptoed over the worn wooden floor. It creaked.

George's eyes flew open. She froze and stared at his flickering eyelids until they drooped shut. By the time she was at the door, he was asleep. On the way to the kitchen, she glanced at the playpen. Junior was in his usual cross-legged pose, awkwardly batting the can of marbles like a kitten chasing yarn. Each time his clenched fists connected with the can, his squeals reached a high pitch. He was growing and his gangly limbs thrashed without warning, making anything in their path vulnerable.

She kept a galvanized tub, rubbing board, and wooden spoon in a corner of the back porch, ready for an explosive diaper or other mishap. Organized baskets of soap cakes and laundry morphed into disorderly piles, no matter how often she seemed to sort them. The laundry loads steadily increased, dirty diapers and towels being the culprits. "Wash day" Monday seeped into "ironing day" Tuesday blurring the remaining days of her week.

She looked at her kitchen, the breakfast dishes already done. Reaching for a towel, she prepared to feed Junior. His bottle sat in a warm pan of water. Heeding the advice of Dr. Edwards, she alternated between a bottle and soft food, feeding him several times throughout the day.

"Are you hungry?" she asked walking closer to his playpen.

His angular head turned toward her voice but his eyes remained shut, tucked away in their concave sockets. Setting the bottle and towel on an end table, she positioned her hands under his armpits. Her muscles tightened as she hoisted him over the playpen rails.

"You're getting big!" she gasped, carrying him to the chair.

His toddler body lay in her lap like a baby. His head

nestled in the crook of her elbow and his legs dangled over her knees. She took his unnaturally curled fingers and wrapped them around the bottle. Pressing her hand tightly over his, her eyes momentarily shut. She held her breath and slowly released her grip. His hands released too.

"**M**uhm."

Ruth whipped her head toward the playpen. Her grip tightened on the broom handle, halting the bristles midsweep against the hardwood floor. She stared at Junior. "What did you say?" she asked.

He sat quietly with the can of marbles on his lap. The Warrior was looking at the ceiling.

She was motionless, except for her hand. It was quietly leaning the broom against the door. "Junior. Did you say something?" she asked.

He remained silent, unmoving in his playpen.

She released the warm handle and inched closer to him. The wooden floor creaked. Her eyes locked on Junior.

"Did you say Mama?"

His fists touched the can of marbles, his crooked fingers rubbed the Warrior label. He picked it up, raising it above his head. The marbles shook loudly with each abrupt movement. She rushed over to the playpen. Squeals burst from his mouth as she swooped him up in her arms.

"You picked up the can!" she cried. "And you said Mama!" She held Junior in the air, laughing and twirling around the living room. She danced and hummed and sang in his ear. She couldn't wait to tell Walter and Dr. Edwards and her mother. But at supper, the conversation didn't go as planned.

"It was probably just one of his mumbles," Walter said.

"No," she said. "He said it. And he picked up the can. I knew he was getting better."

She saw Walter's eyes peering over his soup spoon at her. She set her coffee cup down. It thumped against the kitchen table harder than she anticipated. "I can't wait to hear what Dr. Edwards is gonna say," she said. "Surely, he will have to agree with me now."

"I know what he's gonna say." Walter's words slurped through his soup. "Same as usual."

She turned and faced him. "At least you can hope for the best," she said.

"I do, I do."

She watched as he reached the bread basket filled with his favorite braided loaves. He ripped off a golden section and dunked it into his soup. "Life would be so much easier for me if he was normal," he said.

"For *you*? Try taking care of him. He's growing and getting heavy. He needs my attention for every little thing. And he's still in diapers. Both of them!" she said, waving her hand toward Junior and George.

George waved back.

"Okay, okay," he said. "For you too." He tipped the edge of his bowl to his lips.

"It's not easy, you know." She grabbed the bread basket. "This is more work than two babies."

"I said I know."

The sound of Walter's soup spoon jingling in his empty bowl caused Junior to squeal.

"And," she wagged a piece of bread in the air. "People avoid him. As if he's got the plague. Even Mother."

"Well, you can't really count your mother as people," he said.

"Walter, even you avoid him." She aimed the bread directly at him as he plunged his arm through his coat sleeve.

"I don't avoid him."

"Yes, you do."

"No, I don't."

"Walter. Yes, you do."

"I'm just busy, makin' a livin'. Gotta impress *your* Mother."

She shook her head.

"I'm goin' to Leonard's house," he said.

The sound of the backdoor slamming jolted her. She picked up his bowl and carried it to the sink. She heard the old jalopy sputter to life. The dark car appeared in the kitchen window, slowly backing out of the driveway. The engine roared, then faded. She grabbed a large bowl and put it under the sink faucet. The pipes bumped and howled as a steady stream of hot water poured into the basin. Her soapy hands fumbled for a wet glass when a loud crash sounded behind her.

Shattered on the floor was her coffee cup, scattered throughout the room like stars in the night. Junior and George were quiet, their eyes wide and watching their mother. She stood motionless, hands on her hips, staring at the mess. George's eyes reddened, his face strained. Sobs burst through his opened mouth and Junior began to howl.

Bits of china crunched under her shoes as she walked to the back porch. A row of Walter's clean undershirts hung from a laundry cord in the back room. Searching for a bucket, she lifted one of the shirts. The fabric felt thick and damp. She slid two shirts apart, like a stage curtain. The bucket was sitting near the backdoor, full of dirty water. She cracked the door open and leaned against the door frame.

The night air circled her body and cooled her face as she poured the water out.

Junior squealed as she dropped each china piece into the empty bucket. She dampened a rag and knelt on her hands and knees. With a tilt of her head, she scanned the floor, searching for tiny shards and fragments glistening under the kitchen light. Brown curls stuck to her sweaty forehead as she wiped the floor with large, sweeping circles. She stretched her shoulders and stood up. Junior kept squealing, his fists thrusting through the air and covered in snot. George was smashing a peach slice against his tray. She looked at the table. Junior's can of marbles was in the middle of her chair. The Warrior's eye seemed to be inspecting the room.

14

SHINY GOLD BUTTONS

"Pardon me, ma'am."

Ruth looked at the iceman, standing in the road and stopped her buggy. "Please, go ahead," she said.

A giant block of bluish ice was resting against his back. His hand and wrist bent in an uncanny way, gripping large ice tongs. "Nice day," he said.

"Yes, it is," she answered.

Two easy strides and he was across the sidewalk, making the job of an iceman seem effortless, despite the soggy patches on his clothes.

She pushed the buggy forward. The familiar route to her parent's house brought back childhood memories of hopscotch with Edna and tag with her siblings. The warm summer evenings were her favorite, and after supper, the screen door would fly open, letting her run free with the lazy fireflies. Twilight breathed life into neighborhood campfires where she ate toasted marshmallows, chocolates, and crackers for the first time. Her mouth watered.

Her childhood memories morphed from games and fireflies to courtship strolls with Walter. She remembered chatting about sewing and baking, and Walter explained how machines worked. When she slapped her arm from pesky mosquitos, he removed his jacket to shield her from the nettlesome predators. Every front yard, oak tree, and crack in the sidewalk had a story. The baby buggy was a welcomed addition to her repertoire of events.

Earlier that month, Walter added a seat to the back of the buggy, separating Junior from George. The unsteady, inaugural stroll was marred by a mad dash by Walter and Ruth's dress covered with dirty little footprints. A few pencil sketches later, Walter made the necessary adjustments and the top heavy contraption was balanced.

She adjusted her velvet hat and looked inside the buggy. George was sleeping and Junior was fastened in the back chair. A bird suddenly chirped and a squeal burst from Junior.

"It's okay, Junior," she said.

She gripped the handle and turned a corner. Using Walter's advice for a safe turn, she pushed the handle down, popping the front wheels up and placing the buggy at a different angle. With each wheelie Junior squealed and wiggled but remained tethered to the buggy by an extra strap.

Squinting in the bright daylight, she blinked at a tall woman in the distance. The woman was pushing a buggy toward them and with each step, the gap narrowed. A Hollywood starlet type with a fashionable baby pram was coming her way.

"Edna? Is that you?" Ruth thrust her hand into the air, waving at her childhood friend.

The woman waved back. In a moment, the makeshift two-seater buggy was face to face with a sparkling chrome pram.

Perfume swirled in the air when Ruth embraced her friend. "I didn't know you'd be in town today," she said.

"Norman had an unexpected meeting here. We drove in

last night." Edna's breathy voice sounded the same as it always did, as if the years hadn't passed.

"It's been so long," Ruth said. "Your mother said you had a baby."

Ruth watched as her friend's long, gloved fingers delicately opened the sophisticated pram hood. "Yes," Edna said. "A baby girl."

Ruth looked inside the pram. Shiny gold buttons anchored pink upholstery, puckered yet fluffy, and covering every inch of the interior and nestled in the center was a tiny baby surrounded by silk. Her dainty heart-shaped face peeked out from the luminous material.

"She beautiful," Ruth said.

"Yes," Edna replied, "But she's a handful, and we hired a nanny."

"I've got two boys now and they're a handful, too." Ruth said. She walked to the side of her buggy, blocking Junior from Edna.

"Yes, I've heard," Edna said. The tone of her voice seemed to changed. "You should hire a nanny, make it easier for yourself."

Ruth smiled and nodded. "George is ten months now," she said. "And, here he is."

She pulled at the buddy hood, but it didn't open. Pulling it harder, she wiggled it back and forth, but it still wouldn't budge. She yanked and pushed and jiggled it in every direction, but it would not open. She glanced at Edna and nodded a polite smile. Then, she gripped the hood and gave it a sharp yank, finally setting it free. It dropped to the buggy rim with a clank and a piece of rusted metal fell to the sidewalk. George's eyes squinted at the bright daylight.

"Oh, thank goodness," Edna said. "He's cute."

"Yes, he is," Ruth said and glanced at her friend. "And Edna, this is Junior."

Moving to the back of the buggy, Ruth revealed Junior but kept her hand on his knee.

A sharp gasp escaped her friend. Junior let out a loud grunt, his arms punching the sky.

"He's harmless," Ruth said, grabbing his fists midair. "He's a loving boy, just different, that's all."

Edna stood motionless.

"They're a handful, but they're good boys," Ruth continued, "and smart. Learning every day." Her grip tightened around Junior's arms, but Edna was silent. "He just looks a little different," Ruth said. "But he's smart. Yes, he's smart." She wanted her voice to sound as confident as her mother's, but Edna was backing away from the buggy. "How's Norman's job?" Ruth quickly asked.

"Oh, he's doing well." Edna's words were slowly coming out of her mouth.

"Why don't you and Norman come over for cards tonight?"

"Well, I'm not sure. We have a lot of people to visit, you know how that is," Edna's voice seemed to be fading.

"Maybe this weekend?" Ruth asked.

"No! I mean, well, maybe. I'm not sure. I'll let you know."

"Okay. Well, let's definitively get together before you leave."

"Oh, of course we will."

Edna maneuvered her pram onto the grass, passing Ruth and her buggy.

15

SMALL CIRCLE

Ruth parked the buggy on the sidewalk outside her parents' house. Junior was napping, slumped in his chair. She touched his head. It was sticky and damp and she opened his coat, but he remained asleep. Barricaded under the buggy hood was George. He was sleeping too. She pressed the footbrake that Walter added then gave the buggy a push. It was locked.

"Ruth!"

Her mother's voice was loudly whispering her name. She looked at the front porch. Wearing a flowered print dress and thick oxford shoes, her mother was bounding down the porch steps and heading for the buggy.

"Hello, Mother," Ruth said.

The nudge of her mother's hand pushed her to the front of the buggy. She watched as she glanced up and down the sidewalk. "Let's get him inside," her mother hurriedly whispered.

Unbuckling the seatbelt, Ruth pushed the straps away from Junior's lap. His eyes fluttered open. "Hello, young man," she said.

"Come on," her mother whispered. "Hurry up."

"Okay, okay."

She lifted Junior from the makeshift chair and tried to bring him to her chest but his foot was trapped.

"Hurry," her mother repeated.

Ruth held him in the air, rotating his body in a small circle. She moved him up and down, bending his legs on the seat. He kicked and punched causing her to duck under his swinging fists, but his foot was still trapped.

"What are you caught on?" she asked.

His eyes reddened.

She wriggled his body again and his lips started to tremble.

Her mother grabbed his foot, yanking it from the buggy.

A wail escaped his lungs.

"There," her mother said. She was smiling but her teeth seemed fixed.

Ruth reached for the hidden diaper bag but her mother waved her away. "Quick, get him inside," she said. "I'll get the bag and George."

Inside the house, Ruth sat at the kitchen table with her mother. Sugar crystals slid off the end of her spoon into her coffee. "Yes, Mother, he really said it."

Her mother's kitchen was still the same as the day she married Walter. The counters were clutter free and the windowsill empty, but there was a plate of cookies on the table.

"Are you sure you weren't hearing things?" her mother asked. "Remember how you thought he said ball and he didn't."

"He said an actual word this time," Ruth said. She smoothed George's hair. He was sitting on her lap, cookie in his hand.

"Then why can't he say it now?" her mother asked.

A glass vase sat in the middle of the table. It was the same vase she remembered from childhood. She looked at the reflection. George looked like Junior. "He just doesn't want to talk right now," she said. "That's all."

"Junior," her mother said and pointed at him. He was at the opposite end of the table from her. His lanky legs hung over the foot shelf of an old Victorian highchair, bouncing against the wood. His curled fingers concealed a cookie inside his hands. "Junior," she repeated. "Look at me."

He continued to wiggle and bounce, but he wasn't looking at her.

"Mother, he's getting better," Ruth said. "He's able to pick up things now, and Dr. Edwards said he'd never be able to do that."

"Dr. Edwards said they didn't *know* if he would do that," her mother replied. "They said it was possible, but they weren't sure."

Walter warned her about this visit, saying her mother was going to drill her like a marine sergeant, but she was ready for her mother's questions. "Well," she said, "he's doing a lot that Dr. Edwards didn't know he could do."

"Can he feed himself?" her mother asked.

"Well, no, not yet."

"Than what else can he do?"

Ruth stared at the plate of cookies. The clinking of her mother's spoon against a porcelain coffee cup was the only sound in the kitchen. She pulled George's fingers from his mouth. "How's father?" she asked.

"Your father's fine," her mother replied. "Now back to him."

"Mother, don't start."

"Dr. Edwards said his brain will never develop. And he certainly will not—"

"Mother."

"—talk. You should be thinking about the lunatic asylum. That's where people put their feeble-minded relatives."

"Leave him alone," she said. "He's speaking and getting better. And that's final." She wiped George's gooey finger, hoping he couldn't feel the thumping of her heart. "Is father still working on the weekends?"

"Oh, you know your father, always working. That man doesn't know when to quit. I tell him if he's not home by supper, I will throw his supper away. And yesterday," her mother said, "I did just that."

16

MUDDY GREEN PASTE

"How was your day?" Walter asked.

Ruth cringed at his question. Of all the days for him to be interested, the day spent with her mother was not one of them.

"Fine. How was yours?" she replied.

"Didn't you visit your mother today?" he asked.

She saw his eyes narrow over his newspaper as he looked at her, but she turned away. Junior's bowl of peas needed her attention. She stirred it and stirred it, turning it into muddy green paste.

"Well?" he asked again.

She shoveled the spoon into Junior's mouth.

"Do you really want to know?" she asked.

"Yes," he replied.

She began her story. About how she ran into Edna, and all the questions her mother asked. And how her mother thought she wasn't doing a good job. And how George was probably neglected. And how the asylums know what they're doing. And how Junior needed to be put away. She finished telling him everything, finally looking over at him. But he was reading the newspaper.

"Walter?"

He didn't look up.

Walter."

He shoveled a piece of potato into his mouth, his eyes glued to the newspaper.

"Walter! Did you hear anything I said?" she asked.

His mouth was chewing like a locomotive.

"Walter!"

The side of his mouth cracked open. "What?" he asked.

"What do you think?"

"I don't like your mother."

"Yes, I know that. But what do you think about what she said about the asylum?"

"Maybe she's right," he said. "For a change."

"That's ridiculous."

"Yeah, I know," he said.

17

DIFFERENT DIRECTIONS

Ruth slipped off one of her oxfords. Her toes slid down the back of her heel, removing the other. The living room rug felt warm under her translucent stockings, cradling her feet in wooly fibers. Her foot nudged the hard shoes to the edge of the rug. She looked at George. He was sitting on the floor, leaning against the sofa. His teddy bear in his lap, his little fingers poking at the marble eyes. Then she looked at Junior. He was lying face down on the rug. A snug romper tightly stretched around his bulky diaper, accentuating his bony, protruding limbs. Smashed against the floor was the only pudgy part of his anatomy, his belly.

"Okay, Junior," she said. "You have to move your arms and legs to crawl." She knelt on the floor next to him and rotated his arms then his legs. "Now you try."

His arms swatted the air and his legs kicked back, but his limbs were swimming in different directions, keeping him at a standstill.

"Come on, Junior," she said. "Work together."

He grunted and his limbs thrashed, his tight fist collided with her wrist causing her arm to buckle. She steadied herself and maneuvered one elbow then the other to the ground, letting her body rest next to him.

"Okay, now watch," she said. Pushing her body upward, she slowly crawled forward accentuating each lift of her hand and movement of her knees. She crawled to the end of the rug, turned around and crawled back. "See? Now you try."

He grunted and squealed but did not crawl.

"Crawl, Junior, crawl," she said.

He lay motionless.

She crawled in a circle around his body and came to a halt by his side. Leaning back on her folded knees, she let out a long sigh.

A feathery stroke tickled her foot. Her leg jerked. She turned around to see George behind her with his teddy bear.

18

THE NIGHT STAND

The sound of violent banging woke Walter. He felt the weight of Ruth's body abruptly leave the bed.

"Turn the light on!" she yelled.

Confused, his hand swept the night stand, latching onto the lamp chain.

"Walter!" she shouted. "Help!"

He yanked at the chain. The light turned on, and he looked at Ruth. She was standing over Junior's crib, her arms seemed to be moving in several directions at once. He struggled to put on his glasses, poking his eyes and face, until they slid on. His feet hit the floor and in a moment, he was next to Ruth.

Looking into the crib, he saw Junior. He was blue. His eyes were rolled backward, exposing red, throbbing veins popping through the white. His body was shaking. His arms and legs stiffened and his fists clenched tightly inward.

Ruth wrapped her hands around Junior's head, turning it to the side. Milky spit gurgled out from between his blue lips, his teeth grinding. Shaking and seizing, his three-year-old body was in a continual convulsion.

George burst into a crying fit.

"Let's get him to Dr. Edwards!" Ruth frantically said.

Walter yanked on his pants and threw his coat on over his nightclothes. Scooping Junior into his arms, he rushed to the backdoor. Rain pelted his skin with tiny stings as he shielded Junior from the downpour.

Ruth jumped in the car, yelling for him to place Junior on her lap as she contorted and twisted, positioning George on the backseat.

He ran around the car, hopped in the driver's seat, and pulled the hand brake. He adjusted the levers, pulled the choke, switched the key to battery, and stepped on the starter. The engine whined and chugged, over and over, but didn't start. He lifted his foot off the starter.

"Come on, Betsy," he urged.

"Hurry!" Ruth said.

Water droplets were dripping down his face as he pushed the starter again. The engine whined and whined but still did not start, then went silent. The sound of rain pelting the car roof sounding like a barrage of bullets.

He tried again. Finally, the engine sputtered to life. He pressed the reverse lever and turned toward Ruth. Her toes were tapping the floorboard at a blistering rate and Junior was limp, laying on her lap. Walter rubbed the rain droplets from his glasses and twisted to see out the back. George was in the backseat, his eyes wide, but he was silent.

In a moment, they were on the road.

He squeezed the steering wheel, his foot hovering over the brake pedal and his hand working the acceleration. He squinted out the window, wiping circles through the steam. The windshield wiper raced back and forth struggling to keep up with the night's rain. Skidding to a stop in front of Dr. Edward's house, he pushed the car door open and slung Junior over his shoulder. His feet slid across the wet lawn and up the front porch.

He unleashed a frantic barrage on the front door, then

looked for Ruth. She was racing toward the steps with George tucked in her coat. Rain was splattering her face and she was blinking at a strange pace.

The porch light flicked on. The door slowly opened. Dr. Edwards, in nightclothes, was rubbing his eyes. He fumbled with his glasses, hooking them over his ears.

"Dr. Edwards," Walter said, "something's the matter with my son!"

The sun was peeking above the horizon.

19

SHOCK THERAPY

"What other options do we have?" Walter hoped his voice was as compelling as his words.

Ruth had been sitting in the velvet chair since she put Junior and George down for the evening. He wasn't used to seeing her not working. He crossed the living room.

"I'm taking care of him," she said.

He stopped and looked at her. She didn't seem to be blinking, just staring out the window. He looked out the window too. The theater lights were shining, but the sidewalk was empty.

"I've watched you struggle," he said. "He's only three now. In a few years, it'll be harder."

"It's not a struggle," she said.

He sighed and crossed the room again. "You heard Dr. Edwards. He's gonna have more convulsions. And more often."

"I know."

"Ruth, it's gonna get harder for you."

"I know."

He stopped at the window again. The theater owner was outside, sweeping the sidewalk.

"Maybe we should visit the asylum," he said, "and see for ourselves."

"Wanda's aunt was butchered there. And Dorothy's brother got shock therapy," she said. "And it killed him."

He didn't want his pace to quicken, but it did. "Those are just stories. People say a lot of things that aren't true. Dr. Edwards said they have good doctors and nurses working there. And, they know what they're doin.' "

"But what if the stories *are* true?" Her voice was calm and quiet, but her head was slowly shaking. "I couldn't live with myself if something happened to him."

He stopped and looked at her. She was still staring out the window. He threw his arms in the air. "Okay," he sighed.

A dark red beet rested in Ruth's palm. She was alone in the one room grocery store, except for the shopkeeper, who was standing behind a glowing butcher's case. His knife was cutting fleshy meat off a bone and sawing to the rhythm of Bennie Goodman playing on the radio. She looked at the beet in her hand. Her thumb pressed into the curves of the cold, heavy chard, rubbing pockets of dirt loose and exposing a deep cardinal red. She placed the beet in a small rolling cart. The room was musty and damp, but outside, the sun shined on the warm summer day.

She heard the shopkeeper whistling with the next song. He was loud and off key, but his tempo correct. Pulling a list from her purse, she quickly scanned the scribbled words listing Junior's soft food and other items. She was using the same list from the week before.

Boxes of colorful fruits and vegetables covered long block tables that formed a narrow aisle she had to navigate slowly. Her cart was empty except for three red beets sitting in the upper basket. Tuffs of shaggy stems sprouted from the beet bulbs, like three scalped voodoo heads. She peered out the large glass window into the hazy summer day. Under the awning was the buggy. Junior's legs were bouncing against the seat, securely fastened in his chair, his head bowing from side to side. George was tucked in the back, concealed by the hood. Carefully, she maneuvered the cart toward a box brimming with bright red tomatoes. Rotating a juicy tomato in her hand, she checked it for splits and bruises.

She heard the door jingle open. A large figure caught her eye. It was Mrs. Nowak, one of her mother's friends, and she was heading in her direction.

"Hello, Mrs. Nowak," she said.

"You might want to check your children," she replied.

She leaned around the woman's large frame and looked out the window. The buggy was in the middle of the sidewalk. The hood was lowered and Junior and George were crying. A group of boys had circled them and were pointing and laughing at Junior.

She dropped the tomato and pushed Mrs. Nowak against the vegetable table. Her quick movements attracted the boys' attention, and by the time she reached the front door, the group had disappeared. Grasping the buggy, she pulled George to her chest. Her hand caressed Junior's tear-soaked face, adjusting his fallen suspender.

"Oh, Junior," she whispered.

His cries softened as she touched his cheeks.

She looked up and down the sidewalk. It was empty except for a baseball, rolling to a halt.

"Shame on you!" she said, wagging her finger at the empty street.

Placing George back inside the buggy, she plopped a pacifier in his mouth, then tugged Junior's makeshift seatbelt. She rolled the buggy to the grocery entrance and pushed the door open. The door jingled. Junior squealed and pumped his fists and bounced his legs at the sound. She backed into the store holding the door open with her body.

Grabbing the front end of the buggy, she hoisted it over the two store steps, working it past the solid wooden door. Junior's body lurched backward and forward with each tug. The large buggy filled the doorway as she squeezed around it, making her way outside. She lifted and pushed the heavy contraption over the steps and inside the small store. She smoothed her dress and flicked a loose curl back into place. Mrs. Nowak and the clerk were staring at her. Clearing her throat, she forced a smile. "Is it okay to leave the buggy here?" She asked as politely as she could, motioning to the only open area in the store.

The clerk wiped his bloody hands on his once-white apron and headed toward the door. Inspecting the area around the buggy, he lifted the half-filled gumball machine into the air and placed it against a stack of canned goods. Junior squealed with the rattling gumballs but they were out of his reach.

Nodding her thanks to the clerk, she watched him return to the back of the store before looking inside her cart. The tomato was busted open, oozing juice and seeds over the voodoo beets. She grabbed the cart and pushed it toward a table with berries.

She could see Mrs. Nowak out of the corner of her eye. She was leaning across the counter talking to the clerk. Her murmured words were loud. "That boy needs to be in the asylum. But her mother tells me she's too stubborn to put him in there." In a quieter voice she added, "Such a shame."

Junior let out a loud grunt.

Ruth looked in his direction. His arms were punching the air, but he was safely away from anything in the store.

Mrs. Nowak strutted past her to the front door. "What did you do to that boy? You need to keep him outta sight," she said.

21

COLORFUL MURKY LIQUIDS

"I t's just not possible." Dr. Edwards's voice was detached and lifeless. Ruth looked at his eyes, but they would not meet hers.

A large umbrella lamp hung from the ceiling, flooding the examining room with harsh light. She stood by the metal examining table watching the doctor pat his chest pocket with one hand and hold a clipboard with the other. In the center of the table lay Junior, naked. His eyes were wide and his body motionless. His clenched fists hugged his chest, as if he were in a casket.

"Maybe you didn't hear me," she said. "I said he's crawling."

"Mrs. Janikowski, I heard you. I'm sorry, but that doesn't mean he's cured."

"But you said he would never crawl." Her hand touched Junior's bare shoulder. He flinched.

"No, I said we didn't know if he *could* crawl."

She watched the doctor fiddle with his pen, untwisting the cap.

"But if he's crawling, he could walk, right?" she asked.

"Yes," he said.

"Then he's getting better."

"No. It just means his body is growing. His brain is still an imbecile brain. He will always be an imbecile, a moron." The scratching of his pen on the chart filled the quiet room.

"But I am seeing improvement," she said.

The sound of the pen stopped but he did not look at her. "I'm sorry, Mrs. Janikowski," he said. "It doesn't mean he's getting better."

She looked around the sparsely furnished room. It was bleak and lifeless, like Dr. Edwards's words. A desk, a metal scale, and a glass medicine cabinet edged the walls of the compact space.

"Don't you have something in there that can help him?" she asked. She was studying the medicine cabinet. It was full of tiny glass containers filled with colorful, murky liquids and elixirs.

The clipboard clinked against the empty desk.

She looked at the doctor.

He shuffled to the examining table. "You see the shape of his head?" he asked.

She didn't like the way his pen was pointing at his specimen. "Yes," she replied.

"See his hands?" He grabbed Junior's wrist. Junior flinched. "They're deformed, see?" The doctor dug his pen between Junior's clenched fist. His thin, bony fingers stretched outward, like a roly-poly forced open in the face of danger.

She stared at her son's straightened hand.

The doctor removed his pen. Junior's fingers curled back into a tight fist, cradling against his chest.

"But I'm working with him every day. He is learning."

"I'm afraid that's just wishful thinking," he said. "It's simply not possible. You may be able to care for him now; he's only three, going on four. The convulsions will become more frequent. And violent. He will always need a diaper.

And need to be fed. Basically, he will need help with everything."

She looked at her son. His face was innocent and sweet.

"Now, please," he said. "Think about when he's sixteen, seventeen, and older."

She stared at the doctor. Her eyes began to frantically blink, wishing away a burning sensation.

"Mrs. Janikowski, I think you should consider a mental hygiene institution, an insane asylum. Think of your family."

"But what about the reports?"

"What reports?"

"The reports that people that are butchered and tortured there?"

"Those aren't reports, those are rumors," he said. "And who told you that?"

"People I know. They wouldn't just make that up. People were killed from shock treatment and neglect." She looked at Junior. He was quietly laying on the cold surface, his eyes blinking wide. "No. I don't want him harmed."

"He won't be harmed. I know a few of the doctors working there. They're good. In fact, they're great. They know how to care for idiots and epileptics. And the insane asylum is just down the street from you. You could visit him anytime you wanted."

She searched the doctor's face. His wrinkles pointed downward, his jowls drooping in a permanent scowl but his eyes finally met hers.

"Besides," he said, "that would allow you to properly care for your family and home."

"Are you sure?" she asked.

"Of course. Please, rest assured, an institution is the proper place for your son," he said. "And the sooner, the better."

22

CHANGING

Walter listened to his wife's words, the ones about the asylum and Dr. Edwards. This time, he wondered if their conversation was going to be different.

"He said those reports aren't true," she said.

He stabbed a piece of kielbasa, watching the juice ooze from the pierced skin. He looked across the table. Both his sons were sitting in highchairs. Junior looked like a giant, skinny baby shoved into a small seat, his arms circling high in the air.

"He said we should visit the one down the street," she continued.

Walter plunged the sausage in his mouth, the piece burst with flavor. He had suggested they visit the asylum plenty of times before, but she always said no. "What did you say?" he asked.

"I didn't say anything," she replied.

He stopped chewing and looked at her. It looked like she had thick makeup on her face. But her eyes looked puffy and red.

"You didn't say anything?" he asked, trying to chew casually again.

Her body seemed to stiffen. Her head tipped upward with what looked like a lump sliding down her throat.

"Am I making the wrong decision by keeping him here?" she asked, her eyes were boring into his face.

He swallowed hard, sure that his throat exposed a lump like hers.

"I don't know," he said. "We could have a look, see what they have to offer." He watched her thin fingers move up and down a glass of milk. She brought the glass to her lips, but she didn't drink.

Noises from George drew his attention away from her. George's nose was crinkling, and he was pointing at Junior.

Ruth's nose crinkled too. "I think he needs changing," she said.

Ruth watched Junior's heavy eyelids close. He was sitting on her lap. His pink lips were twitching and clinging to his binky. The stagnant summer humidity stifled the massive church despite the stained glass windows angling open to the outside world. She looked at the tightly packed pews in front of her. The perspiring parishioners were fanning their missals at a feverish pace. She touched Junior's face. It was sweaty. Wiping damp hair from his forehead, she shifted her knees into the empty seat next to her and moved Junior to a dry area on her lap. A puff of air from Walter's moving missal passed her face causing a temporary warm breeze. She looked at her husband. George was curled against his shoulder, his arms dangling loosely around Walter's neck. A deep organ note vibrated from the church balcony. She rubbed Junior's arm. Then another note sounded, and another. A religious melody of sharps and flats bellowed from the large golden pipes dominating the crowded church.

She placed her arms over Junior's sleeping body, preparing for an abrupt awakening. But he remained asleep. A breeze circulated around the back pew, whispering over her neck. She watched the usher scan her row, eyeing the fragmented section next to her. An altar boy peeked out from the vestibule and glanced at the audience. The golden crucifix he was holding was taller than he was, and it tipped forward as he searched the crowd. He was steadying the cross when a hand grabbed his shoulder, pulling him back into the small room.

The organ paused.

She saw her parents rush in. She waved, catching their attention and motioning them to the empty seats next to her. Her father started to walk toward her but her mother's hand brought him to a halt. Her mother mouthed the words, "We'll see you after church," and tugged her father to a pew near the altar.

With a loud reverberating organ note, a new song began and the congregation rose to their feet, but, she remained seated, rocking Junior in her lap. She looked at the entrance. The tall crucifix entered the aisle, swaying in the altar boy's hands as he struggled to keep it upright. He was followed by two more altar boys and the priest.

She glanced up at Walter. He was studying the procession, with George snuggled to his chest. She smiled. Last Sunday, Walter said he was staying home from church. She tried to convince him to attend.

But he had said, "Church isn't a place for somebody like me."

She said she couldn't manage the two boys by herself for the entire mass and suggested Junior stay home with him. She assured Walter that Junior would be asleep in no time, and he would have the house to himself. But when she returned, she found Walter's Brylcreem hair as fuzzy as a coconut, his glasses cockeyed, and he was missing a shoe. The sofa was littered with bits of peaches, an array of Walter's hats were scattered on the floor, and a paper airplane was taped to a flyswatter. In the kitchen, a small footprint had appeared in a glob of mashed peaches, and a broken pencil was soaking in Walter's coffee cup. Ruth's mouth hung open.

Walter proudly announced, "I did it! I got him to sleep."

Today, as the congregation took their seats, she watched Walter rubbing George's back. The service began. Smoke from a swinging incense thurible snaked around the room, heating the already warm space. The crowd spoke in unison and sung in mixed voices with a gothic-sounding choir. By the time the communion rite began, she expected Junior to wake, but he remained peacefully asleep. Row by row, parishioners slowly stood, exiting their pews, wandering as if in an endless maze. Each person approached the priest with bowed head, then returned to their rightful seat. Eventually the circular line dwindled. The row in front of Ruth stood up. She watched Junior. His mouth quietly twitched, his eyes remained closed. The communion procession ended. The priest bowed his head to the seated congregation and concluded the communion rite. Then he returned to his throne and sat in prayer. She glanced at Walter, who was still rubbing George's back. Bowing her head, she closed her eyes.

The massive room was silent.

A loud grunt escaped Junior. His head jerked upward, whacking her chin. His cacophonous squeals pierced the quiet church. Simultaneously, heads snapped awake. She hastily covered his mouth but his head wiggled and squirmed breaking free from her grasp. Her arm tightened around his body and her hand found his mouth again, but his arm snuck loose. It swung wildly, hitting George in the head and knocking Walter's glasses to the floor. A high pitched wail sailed upward from George. Junior screeched and grunted, fighting with her hold. She struggled to control his body, but his arms and legs lashed in different directions and she couldn't keep up. All eyes turned toward the back row. An old lady sitting in front of Walter scowled, holding one finger over her lips as she hissed at Junior.

Junior's animal grunts were getting louder and mixing with George's howling. She frantically gathered their belongings, stuffing everything into her bag and stood up. She saw Walter leaning toward the floor, his fingers hooking on to his glasses when Junior kicked his head.

"Ow!" he yelped. His shirt was soaked with sweat.

Clenching the worn pew, she positioned Junior on her hip and slid toward the side aisle. "Pardon me," she said, stepping around knees of parishioners sandwiched at the end of the row. Junior's arms and legs punched and kicked on their way out, sending heads lurching backward.

Outside she gasped for air as she calmed Junior down. Moments later, Walter and George joined them. Walter loaded the buggy in silence. The church doors swung open and the crowd poured outside. She watched the departing group.

"Come on," Walter said.

"But my mother." She looked at Walter. "She said she'd see me after church."

He did not stop. "Come on," he repeated. "She's not coming out anytime soon."

She scanned the crowd.

Her parents were nowhere in sight.

24

A NORMAL MAN

At the factory, Walter was a normal man. Although the days were long and the line was grueling, he fit in there. He knew he was popular and funny, entertaining his co-workers with jokes and stories. Everybody liked him. When Junior was born, friends and family praised his first born son, excited to meet his namesake. He had a permanent smile on his face. But that quickly changed. Soon, he felt rejected. Shunned by the same people that slapped his back and offered congratulatory cigars.

Junior scared him.

The looks on people's faces said it all. Ruth would set Junior on the front porch in his playpen, the cars his entertainment. She tried to make Junior normal. She tried to make a happy family. But he was ashamed. Ruth said Junior would be fine. He was learning every day. But he didn't see any improvement.

He's three years old, for Christ's sake.

If anything, the older Junior became, the more obvious it was that things weren't right. His arms and legs became thinner and bonier. His clenched fists closely guarded his chest. And his fingers. His curled fingers that looked like two haunted trees moving slowly in the wind. And he couldn't speak. Only grunts, like an animal. And his skull. His misshaped skull. Almost Frankensteinish.

He knew people blamed Ruth.

He knew her mother blamed him too, because he was a peasant.

PART III

1946

There is none
In all this cold and hollow world, no fount,
Of deep, strong, deathless love, save that within
A mother's heart.
— FELICIA HEMANS

"You're tracking dirt inside."

George stopped and looked at his mother. She was standing at the kitchen sink, one hand holding a ladle, the other pointing to a trail of mud starting at the backdoor and leading to his shoes. He plopped his school books on the table and scanned the kitchen counter. It was empty except for a chopping board full of carrot tops and celery leaves. He untied one shoe and let it drop to the floor.

"I just mopped," she said. "Why aren't you leaving your shoes at the backdoor?"

Her belly was getting big. He wasn't sure if he wanted a brother or sister, or anyone at all. Anna already took up a lot of his time. His six-year-old sister was annoying and always asking him questions.

"He's just gonna get it dirty anyways," he replied.

He looked at Junior who was sitting with his back against the locked pantry door. A loud, powerful grunt filled the kitchen. He was two years older than George. Twelve to his ten. He had a growth spurt over the summer and his abnormally gaunt body made his tall frame appear even taller. His angular, misshapen head and bony limbs mirrored the image of the malnourished foreigners he was learning about in class. Sometimes Junior's arms would swing wildly, knocking over something or hitting George when he wasn't looking. Despite his spindly body, he was strong.

"How did you get so much dirt on your shoes?" she asked.

"I dunno," he said. He hobbled and danced on a shoeless foot, fighting with a stubborn knot.

On the stove, a lid to a large pot clattered, clashing with the rattles from Junior's can of marbles. A lopsided pot holder that Anna made was bunched up in his mother's hand. He watched her pick up the lid and lean into a billowing cloud of steam. The clattering stopped but the jingling of the marbles became louder and an aroma of garlic filled the room. He dropped his second shoe to the floor. His mother turned and looked at him.

"Get the broom and clean this up before you go upstairs," she said. "I've got to feed him."

He was sick of doing chores.

"Do we have any cookies?" he asked.

"I haven't had time to make any. Now clean this up."

He stomped to the back porch. The room was warm and dry. Afternoon sunlight shined in the tiny space exposing dust particles floating in the air, like their own little universes. He couldn't find the broom, and he wasn't going to look very hard. He walked back into the kitchen. The trail of mud flakes crunched under his feet and were sticking to his socks.

Junior's sunken eyes were looking around the room, seemingly at nothing, when suddenly, they stopped and stared straight at him.

"What?" George said, knowing his brother wouldn't answer.

Junior's arms flew up in the air, his feet kicked forward and pushed the can across the room. The can rolled slowly, the Warrior's eye watching the ceiling, then the floor, then the ceiling, coming to rest against his mother's slipper. "I know, I know," she said. "I'm getting your bottle ready."

His mother was constantly helping Junior with every little thing. He wished Junior could help himself. She was cradling her stomach as she bent down to pick up the can. The closer she walked to Junior, the quicker his arms and legs bounced. She placed the can in front of him. His fists batted at his toy, rolling it back and forth between his bent legs.

"Where's your sister?" she asked, walking to the living room doorway.

He shrugged.

"Anna!" she yelled. "Wash your hands and do your chores."

The house was quiet. His mother's voice usually had a way of getting attention but there was no sound from the second floor. He knew Anna was upstairs. She didn't want to do her chores either.

"Anna?" His mother called her a second time.

The muffled sound of Anna's voice drifted to his ears. He couldn't hear what she was saying, but he knew his sister wasn't coming downstairs.

"Come down here and do your chores."

Silence.

"Now!" she yelled.

He heard Anna scampering from the second floor as his mother returned to the kitchen. Junior was shuffling toward the clattering pot on the stove.

"Junior, sit," she said. "George, you need to watch your brother."

Her hand touched Junior's elbow causing him to flinch.

"Sit," she repeated, pointing to the floor.

His head wobbled back and forth. His eyes fluttered. George wondered if that was his way of getting out of doing what his mother asked.

"Sit," she said, her voice becoming softer. Junior finally sat with a plop. "Now, sweep this floor, George."

"I can't find the broom."

"It's where it always is," she said. "Next to the door."

He was headed back to the porch when she added, "And go get your sister."

"Which one do you want me to do first?"

"Get Anna, please."

His foot nudged the can of marbles as he stomped toward the living room. He gripped the stair cap ready to pull his body upward but his sister was on the top step, heading down.

"You better get down here," he said. "Or you're gonna get in trouble."

"I know." Anna's face scrunched, just like when she eats lemons.

He walked into the kitchen, slipping around Junior. He felt Anna close behind him.

"You're too close," he said.

"No, I'm not."

He looked at the counter. "I'm hungry."

"Me too," Anna said.

"Your father will be home soon. Now get your chores done."

George felt a whack on the back of his leg. "Ow!" he said. He turned around and saw Junior swatting at the air.

"Anna, go get a rag," his mother said. "And George, sweep this floor!"

He followed his sister to the back porch.

"I should make you do *my* chores," she whispered. "You owe me one."

"For what?"

"Last night," she said. "You told Ma you were doing your homework when you were really playing with those stupid airplanes."

"Shhh," he said as he thought about last night.

When his father converted the second-floor attic, he had first choice of rooms. He was younger then, but picking the room in the back was an easy decision because it was away from the racket below. Junior had a way of finding his toys and pencils and breaking each one. For his birthday this year, a long, thin box wrapped in newspaper was waiting for him at the breakfast table. The coveted Grumman F6F Hellcat was inside. He spent hours alone in his room, penciling detailed designs and constructing miniature balsa airplanes. He glued and tacked and cut the small-scale pieces far away from his brother's flailing arms. At night, the light from the back yard shined into his room, his hanging airplanes casted large shadows on his ceiling, and he sat on his bed, playing pilot.

He returned to the kitchen, and Anna was right behind him.

"Is this one good?" Anna asked, holding out a rag.

"Yes," his mother said. "Now dust the living room, please."

He didn't think his mother even looked at the rag. She was busy feeding Junior his bottle. He tapped the broom against the floor, aiming the bristles at a big piece of dirt.

What's on your hand?" she asked.

He looked at his knuckles. They were scraped.

"Nothin'," he replied.

She stood up and placed Junior's bottle on the counter and walked over to him.

He looked at the floor, slowly sweeping the dirt into a pile.

She pulled his arm toward her.

"How did you get these scrapes?" she asked.

"Playing ball." He yanked his hand out of hers and continued sweeping.

Putrid stink filled his nose, replacing the garlic.

He looked at Junior. His face was grimacing as he swatted at the can of marbles.

"I think he pooped," George said.

The can was rolling across the floor. George used the broom like a hockey stick to stop the Warrior and swatted the can like a puck, directly into the lower cabinets.

"George!" his mother yelled. "Pick it up and give it back to him."

He stomped to the cabinets and placed the broom bristles against the can.

Junior reached for the broom handle.

"Don't!" he said and picked up the broom, holding it over Junior's head.

"Stop it, George! He doesn't know what he's doing."

"I hate him!" he yelled. "He's feeble minded!"

"What? Where did you hear that?"

He wished he hadn't said that, especially to his mother.

"George! Where did you hear that?" she repeated.

He stayed silent.

"George?" Her voice was quieter but her face was closer to his.

He looked at the floor. His eyes were burning. He felt the touch of her hand on his shoulder as she asked him again.

"At school," he replied. Then added, "They say I'm feeble minded, too."

He kept his gaze on his mother's slippers. He didn't want to look at her face. She was sad enough.

"Look at me," she said.

He stayed focused on her feet. Her ankles were swollen and there was a stain on one of her slippers.

"Look at me," she repeated.

Slowly he lifted his head. Tear droplets were clinging to his eyelashes, making his mother's face blurry.

"I know this is hard," she said. "He *is* different. People don't understand, but *you* can."

26

T he tapping noises from George's bedroom warned Anna to stay away. Lectures on the Piper Cub, Curtiss P-40 Warhawk, or the Avenger, better known as the Torpedo Bomber did not impress her.

She remembered the day her father suspended wires from the corners of his room, a few days after his birthday. The airplanes looked like they were flying. And one summer night, she heard the floorboards creak in her brother's room. She tiptoed down the hall and peeked inside. He must've climbed out his window because he was sitting on the back porch rooftop, sitting and staring at the stars. She knew he wasn't supposed to do that, but she never told anybody about it either.

Her room was at the front of the house and she cherished it. The front window gave her a bird's-eye view to the glitzy theater below and a built-in dresser formed the perfect perch. On weekend nights, she would grab her thick quilt, climb up the drawers and create a cozy nest, away from Junior's fuss and trouble below. She loved watching the fashionable movie goers laughing and talking as they stood in line for their tickets. She imagined the movies within and the actors and actresses on screen. Some nights, if she woke up in time, she would see Frank, the owner, turning the lights off and locking the doors. He would walk into the dark night picking up trash from the sidewalk, then disappear around the corner.

She was glad Junior didn't come upstairs. She loved him, but he was always making a mess.

27

BOTTOM OF THE STAIRS

H is mother twisted the black telephone cord around her fingers. "I'll only be gone twenty minutes," she said. "Maybe even less."

George stood at the top of the stairs. His hand gripped the railing as the words drifted upward.

"To the market," she continued. "It won't take me long."

Listening to his mother's anxious voice made his throat dry. Her shoes clicked against the wooden floor as she paced.

"Just this once," she said. "I'm out of baby food."

He let his foot hover over the first step but he didn't step down.

"No, he won't have a convulsion."

Quietly, he landed on the top step.

"Because I know, Mother," she said. "Irene will be down for a nap and George and Anna will be upstairs doing their homework."

The clicking of her shoes sounded again. This time, she walked too far away from the tiny stand the telephone rested on, almost tipping it over.

"He'll be in the pantry. You won't have to do anything, just be here."

George thought of the pantry, now Junior's room. A few years back, his father removed the shelves and converted the small space into a room for Junior with a custom bed big enough for his brother's growing body. A second door leading to his parent's bedroom was added, and a lock was placed on the door to the kitchen. After the first bumpy nights, his mother lined the walls with thick padding, and his father added an adjustable bed rail to keep his brother from falling out. He hated the mornings when he heard his mother scurrying out of bed and into the pantry. He knew Junior was having another convulsion.

"Alright, maybe next time," his mother said and hung up the telephone.

He was at the bottom of the stairs. "Ma?" he whispered.

Her head jerked up.

"Is Busia coming over?"

"No," she replied.

"I can watch him," he said.

His mother placed her hand on his shoulder. Her touch was soft. She smiled at him, but her eyes were filled with sadness.

"Thank you, George, but you're too young."

"I'm almost eleven!"

She shook her head.

"Then I'll go to the store for you," he said.

28

WHITE SMOKE

A stubby cigar poked out of Walter's mouth. Ruth watched the ashy end flash bright red. She was standing next to a tiny heater in his workshop, a coffee cup in hand, but she was cold.

"What kind of life does he have?" he asked. One side of his lips moved, the other side clung to a cigar.

She looked at the drawings on his work table. Angles and squares and scribbled writing filled the paper. "What are those pencil sketches of?" she asked.

She heard him sigh and looked at his face. He was staring at her. His index finger hooked around his cigar, pulling it out with a little pop. His eyes glanced at the drawings, then back to her face. His head tilted back and his mouth parted. A thin line of white smoke slithered into the air.

"Ruth," he said. "All he does is shake those marbles."

She heard the tone of his voice. It sounded exhausted, just like she felt.

"Maybe we should just go look at the asylum," he continued. "See for ourselves."

She heard all this before. The conversation was not new.

Her house was neglected. George and Anna were neglected and Irene was left in her playpen most of the day. There was no help. Junior absorbed every moment of her time, even in her sleep. She justified locking him in the pantry to allow her time to get something done, anything. He liked to shake the Warrior, to hear the marbles rattle against the tin can. His high pitched squeals told her that much.

"I know what you're going to say," he said, "but hear me out. The people that run these asylums, the doctors and nurses, they're trained to take care of people like him. Dr. Edwards has told you that a hundred times. Remember?"

She looked at her coffee. Various shades of brown swirled like a liquid pinwheel with the slightest movement.

"Why, just the other day," he said, "one of the fellas at work was talkin' about how his wife's sister's in there. And she's getting better. He was sayin' his wife is happier now that she doesn't have all that responsibility. And she visits her sister anytime she likes."

She raised the cup to her lips.

"Ya know, Junior is only twelve," he said. "And he's strong. It won't be long before you won't be able to control him anymore, like when he walked out the front door into the street. And how will you change his diaper?"

She sipped her coffee. The bitter, nutty flavor offered a tiny moment of peace.

"Besides," he said, "he can't sit in the pantry all day, that's what the asylum's for. Then you'll have more time for the kids. And me. Besides, don't you want a normal life again?"

A normal life. Would she even know what that was? She sat down on the work bench. Her eyes felt heavy.

"Let's just go for a visit," he said. "Have a look around. We don't have to commit to anything. Just look."

She released a long, deep breath. "Maybe you're right," she said.

T he priest's hand raised over the congregation. "The Mass has ended, go in peace," he said.

Ruth joined in the customary response with the other parishioners. The organ pipes began to bellow. A moment later, the choir joined in. She adjusted Irene's baby bonnet and snuggled her to her shoulder. Anna's angelic singing voice floated to her ears, but the off key voices from the surrounding pews seemed to drown her out. Ruth looked at George, he was standing on the other side of her and seemed to be in a daydream. She nudged his arm. He began to mouth the words to the song, but there was no sound coming out.

At the altar, a disorganized group of altar boys surrounded the priest. Even though their mouths were moving, she was sure there was no sound coming out either. She gazed at a giant crucifix hanging behind the boys. It was framed in a gilded arch topped with detailed golden spirals spiking upward.

The closing procession had begun.

She felt a tug on the missal in her hand. Anna pulled it free and stuffed it into the booklet pouch on the pew.

Another song began, a peppy church march, and the parishioners started to leave.

George and Anna ducked into the crowded aisle in front of her. She heard conversations about the spring weather and the upcoming Easter holiday. People were compressed together, shuffling down the aisle when she felt her coat sleeve move. A warm hand tugged at her elbow. She turned around. Mrs. Kowalski stood there, smiling at her.

"I'm glad I found you," she said.

They walked together to the end of the aisle. Ruth dipped her fingertips into the bowl of holy water and dabbed her forehead, chest, and each shoulder. Her fingers dipped a second time, and she touched the top of Irene's head.

The crowd thinned, emptying into the spring day.

Mrs. Kowalski walked with her to the sanctuary and the open doors. Ruth was about to step outside when she felt the woman's hand land on her arm.

"I wanted to see how you're doing," she said.

Ruth stopped and looked outside at the church steps. The priest was greeting the last of his flock. George and Anna were outside too, looking at something on the sidewalk.

"How is everything going?" Mrs. Kowalski asked.

She thought about the question as she watched one remaining family milling in the church yard. They were smiling and laughing as if they had not a care in the world.

"Are you okay?" Mrs. Kowalski asked.

She forced a smile. "Yes, how are you?"

"I'm fine," she answered. "How's Junior?"

She looked at Mrs. Kowalski. The blue in her eyes was the same color as Junior's. "Am I making a mistake?" she asked.

The blood in Mrs. Kowalski face seemed to disappear, making the blue even brighter.

"People keep saying that he should be in the asylum, that's what's best for him," she continued. "But I'm taking good care of him. It's difficult and I know it will get harder, but—" she stopped, before adding, "maybe I've been wrong all along."

Mrs. Kowalski's posture shifted, she straightened her hunched back. "I don't know how to tell you this," she said. "But, I heard *another story*."

An overwhelming need to run flooded Ruth.

"I know you don't want to hear this," Mrs. Kowalski continued, "but I think you should know."

Ruth looked at the doors. They were wide open, and if she hurried, she could run away.

"Do you remember Mildred Dubicki? Mrs. Mildred Dubicki?" Mrs. Kowalski asked. "Her son, Thomas, is a few years older than you and Edna. Do you remember her?"

She nodded but she didn't want to hear anymore.

"Well—" Mrs. Kowalski abruptly stopped.

One of the ushers stepped inside. "Mornin' ladies," he said.

"Good morning," Mrs. Kowalski responded.

"Sure is nice today," he said. He released the brass door stops.

"Yes, it is," Mrs. Kowalski replied.

The doors slowly closed. The room darkened. Ruth's vision seemed hazy and dreamlike.

"Would you ladies be more comfortable in the church?" he asked.

Mrs. Kowalski looked at her.

Ruth shook her head.

"No, we're fine," Mrs. Kowalski said. "Thank you."

"Suit yourself," he said and left.

"Mildred Dubicki, do you remember her?"

Mrs. Kowalski was going to tell her the story whether she wanted to hear it or not.

"Well, her sister was having some trouble after her husband died. You know, upset, crying all the time. Well, they put her in the asylum hoping they would be able to help her. She was released a few months later with two black eyes."

Ruth wasn't sure what she was saying anymore.

"Some new procedure," Mrs. Kowalski whispered. "A lah-bah-toe-me. Or something like that. They push a sharp instrument into the eye socket and tap it into the brain. Then they scramble it."

A metallic taste filled Ruth's mouth.

"It was supposed to help her mood," Mrs. Kowalski said. "There was a doctor from Washington, teaching at the asylum. He did it. And when they got her home, she didn't say anything. They kept asking her questions, but she didn't speak. Couldn't do anything. Now they say she just sits and drools."

30

THICK BLACK CORD

"Time for bed!" Ruth called from the kitchen. Her fingers looped around the faucet knob, turning the steaming water flow off. The pipes went quiet. The last bowl was washed and leaning against a stack of drying dishes as she stood still and listened for movement from the living room. The house was silent, almost peaceful. "Time for bed!" she repeated.

The clean dishes gleamed under the kitchen light as she picked up a towel and began to dry. A hot puff of breath moistened the back of her neck and a sour smell circled her nose. She turned around. Junior was standing behind her.

"No, Junior," she said. "Back to the living room."

He didn't move. A low quiet grunt emerged from his throat. He shuffled closer to the sink.

She set the towel down.

Junior put his hands inside the basin and slapped at the bubbles at the bottom of the sink.

"Come on, Junior," she said.

Her damp hands rubbed the rough cotton of her apron, then wrapped around his arms. She pulled him from the sink but he was resisting her.

"Come on," she repeated.

The more she pulled, the more his body contorted and bent backward.

"Let's get you back to the living room," she said.

His socked feet slid across the kitchen floor and into the living room.

"Now, sit," she said.

Pushing on his shoulders and using her foot to bend his knees, she maneuvered his body to the floor.

She looked around the room. Anna was stretched over the worn area rug and a collection of pencils and papers were scattered around her. George was lying on the sofa, a book raised above his head, and his lips were silently moving.

Nudging Junior, she pushed him against the sofa. He was sucking his preadolescent thumb and staring at the other side of the room.

"Anna," she said. "Pick up your pencils and get to bed."

Her daughter hummed as she wiggled a stubby, broken pencil.

"Quit humming," George said. "I'm trying to read."

"Anna," Ruth repeated. "Time for bed."

She returned to the kitchen. Milk glass rings covered the table, along with food crumbs and her coffee cup. Grabbing the dish rag, she squeezed the remaining water out and wiped the food remnants. The gooey mess gathered to the edge of the table and into her ladled palm. She thought of her next chore and walked to the back porch. The room was dark. She flipped the light switch, but the light did not turn on. She flicked it a few more times, but the room remained unlit. Squinting, she spotted the ironing board leaning against a cabinet. She shuffled and nudged dirty towels out of her pathway and reached for the cumbersome board. She dragged it into the kitchen then returned to the porch.

Unlocking a cabinet door, she peered into the dark

cavity. A silver iron reflected what little light was in the room. She carried it into the kitchen, its heavy cord trailing behind like a baby's blanket.

"Anna," she called out, "put your pencils away."

"Okay, Ma."

The metal legs of the ironing board screeched open. Junior's squeals drifted into the kitchen. Removing Walter's homemade electrical cover, she plugged the thick black cord into the socket, then glanced into the living room. Anna's pencil was still moving.

"Anna. Bed. Now!"

The pencil dropped. Anna's fingers splayed over her drawings, gathering them into a pile.

"Don't forget your pencils," Ruth added. "All of them this time."

"I won't."

She watched as Anna plucked the pencils from the floor and stood up. Her outstretched arm centered over a bean can, dropping each pencil with a clank. Ruth spotted Junior, he seemed to be watching Anna, too. The higher Anna's arm raised, the louder the pencils jingled and the more he squealed and wiggled.

"Anna!" she yelled. "Get moving."

"I am. Don't forget my dress," Anna replied.

"Working on it now."

Ruth licked her finger and dabbed the iron. It sizzled. Fluffing Anna's dress over the ironing board, she patted the material down. The iron felt heavy as she slowly moved it over the dress.

A loud crash sounded from the living room.

She dropped the iron and ran into the room. A photo of her parents in a glass picture frame lay shattered on the floor. Standing in the broken glass was Junior, yelping and screaming.

She moved him out of the mess and grabbed his hands.

"George!" she said. "Why weren't you watching your brother?"

Junior was whimpering as she looked at his palms.

"How did he reach this picture?"

"I dunno," George answered. "I was doing my homework."

"Grab the waste basket," she said. "And bring the dust pan, too."

Junior was licking his fingers.

"Junior," she said, "sit down."

He wandered to the other side of the living room.

She squatted and gathered the large pieces of glass. George set the waste basket down by her knees.

"Watch your step," she said.

Tapping the dust pan against the basket, she leaned closer to the floor. A deafening scream sounded from the back of the house. She sprung up and dashed into the kitchen.

Junior was standing near the ironing board blowing on his hand.

"Junior!" she yelled.

His fingertips were bright pink and his arms were shaking.

She pulled him to the sink.

"What's going on?" Walter asked, coming in from the back door.

31

POISED LIKE A DOLL

Ruth heard the mailbox lid screech open earlier than usual. Her hand paused over the washboard. She felt a bead of sweat trickling down her temple as she strained to hear the mailman's footsteps on the front porch. Instead, she heard the muffled sound of Junior's marbles. Clutching the soapy brush, she wiped her brow, watching droplets of soap and sweat splash into the washtub. The stain on Junior's pants was almost gone. She stood up. Grabbing the front of her apron, she searched for a dry patch and eyed the mound of dirty laundry that didn't seem any smaller.

She passed the sink full of dishes and stepped over a book. The living room was quiet and so was the bedroom. She peeked at Irene, asleep in Junior's old crib, then pressed her ear to the closed pantry door. Junior's can of marbles stopped.

She exited the room quickly and opened the front door. A satiny treasure poked out of the mailbox. She grabbed at the glossy magazine that contained stories about world events and world leaders, actors and actresses, and photography—the beautiful, engaging photography that showed her another world. She rarely let her weekly indulgence hit the bottom of the mailbox, instead, the mailman usually placed it in her waiting hand. The magazine felt cool and silky in her calloused hands. She tossed the remaining mail on the dusty desk and sunk into the velvet chair. The magazine rested on her lap as her fingers clutched the edges.

Life Magazine. May 6, 1946.

Her hand slid up and down the smooth, sophisticated cover. Margaret Leighton was wearing a theatrical, floor-length dress, forever suspended in black and white. Attached to a cloth circlet was a medieval veil wrapped tightly under her chin and her delicate hands were poised like a doll's.

She opened the magazine. A dreamy blue advertisement filled the first page. A newlywed couple was cutting their wedding cake, teaching young women that the finest silver-plated utensils were essential for a happy life. She touched the ad. The opposite page showcased treads on a new tire, stating how they can outwear prewar tires. Her eyes bounced from one ad to the other, and back again. She turned the page. Ads for crisp apple juice, optical wardrobes, the latest refrigerator, and nylon stockings fed her eyes. She read of hunger haunting Europe, skipped the Dodgers article, studied the new shade of nail enamel and frowned at her own cracked fingernails. She read and reread the etiquette article, sure her mother was scrutinizing the same one. The rattle of Junior's marbles interrupted the moment. She strained to hear anything unusual, but everything was quiet. Setting the magazine aside, she headed to the pantry door and opened it. Junior was sitting on his bed rattling the can. She looked around the small space, sniffing the air. The room smelled fine.

Settling back into the chair, she picked up the magazine. A debutant gets married. The dream house of the future. The London Theater visits the US, but the black and white photographs of Shakespearean actors caught her attention. She bent a page corner, earmarking a possible Halloween costume for George that had a sword she was sure he would love. She leafed through a few pages searching for a costume idea for Anna. Then, she turned the page. A downtrodden, barefooted woman strapped in a straitjacket was sitting alone, her face hidden, her legs wounded.

Ruth began to read the article.

"THIS WOMAN WEARS A CAMISOLE WITH SLEEVES
TIED BEHIND HER. ULCERS ON HER LEGS ARE
UNBANDAGED" Photo Credit 1: *by Jerry Cooke © 2019 Jerry Cooke
Archives*

Source of material:
From the pages of
LIFE

Bedlam, 1946

MOST U.S. MENTAL HOSPITALS ARE A SHAME AND A DISGRACE

by Albert Q. Maisel

In Philadelphia the sovereign Commonwealth of Pennsylvania maintains a dilapidated, overcrowded, undermanned mental "hospital" known as the "Dungeon," one can still read, after nine years, the five-word legend, "George was killed here, 1937."

This pitiful memorial might apply quite as well to hundreds of other Georges in mental institutions in almost every state in the Union, for Pennsylvania is not unique. Through public neglect ad [sic] legislative penny-pinching, state after state has allowed its institutions for the care and cure of the mentally sick to degenerate into little more than concentration camps on the Belsen pattern.

Court and grand-jury records document scores of deaths of patients following beatings by attendants. Hundreds of instances of abuse, falling just short of manslaughter, are similarly documented. And reliable evidence, from hospital after hospital, indicates that these are but a tiny fraction of the beatings that occur, day after day, only to be covered up by a tacit conspiracy of mutually protective silence and a code that ostracizes employees who sing too loud."

Yet beatings and murders are hardly the most significant of the indignities we have heaped upon most of the 400,000 guiltless patient-prisoners of over 180 state mental institutions…

We feed thousands a starvation diet, often dragged further below the low-budget standard by the withdrawal of the best food for the staff dining rooms. We jam-pack men, women and sometimes even children into hundred-year-old firetraps in wards so crowded that the floors cannot be seen between the rickety cots, while thousands more sleep on ticks, on blankets, or on the bare floors. We give them little and shoddy clothing at best. Hundreds — of my own knowledge and sight — spend twenty-four hours a day in stark and filthy nakedness…

Thousands spend their days — often for weeks at a stretch — locked in devices euphemistically called "restraints": thick leather handcuffs, great canvas camisoles, "muffs," "mitts," wristlets, locks and straps and restraining sheets. Hundreds are confined in "lodges" — bare bedless, rooms reeking with filth and feces — by day lit only through half-inch holes though steel-plated windows, by night merely black tombs in which the cries of the insane echo unheard from the peeling plaster of the walls.

Worst of all, for these wards of society we provide physicians, nurses and attendants in numbers far below even the minimum standards set by state rules. Institutions that would be seriously unmanned even if not overcrowded find themselves swamped with 30%, 50% and even 100% more patients than they were built to hold…

"…The testimony revealed that these four attendants slapped patients in the face as hard as they could, pummeling in their ribs with fists, some being knocked to the floor and kicked. One 230-pound bully had the habit of bumping patients on the back of the head with the heel of his hand — and on one occasion had the patient put his hand on a chair, the striking his fingers with a heavy passkey…"

From a state hospital in Iowa comes the following report: "Then the 'charge' (attendant) and the patient who had done the choking began to kick the offender, principally along the back, but there were several kicks at the back of the neck and one very painful one in the genitals which caused the victim to scream and roll in agony. … Sometimes more than 20 kicks must have been administered. Finally he was dragged down the floor and locked in a side room. When I asked the 'charge' how it started, he said 'Oh, nothing. That — — — — ought to be killed.' The victim was in handcuffs all the time; had been in handcuffs continuously for several days."

From an Ohio state hospital: "An attendant and I were sitting on the porch watching the patients. Somebody came along sweeping and the attendant yelled at a patient to get up off the bench so that the worker-patient could sweep. But the patient did not move. The attendant jumped up with an inch-wide restraining strap and began to beat the patient in the face and on top of the head. 'Get the hell up…!' It was a few minutes — a few horrible ones for the patient — before the attendant discovered that he was strapped around the middle to the bench and could not get up."

33

POUNDED SHUT

Ruth scoured the bathroom floor. Next she scrubbed Junior's dirty diapers, all of them. After that she got out a ladder from Walter's workshop and dusted the crown molding. The house was clean, very clean, but the magazine was still there. It was in the garbage can, outside, with the lid pounded shut. After ironing the bedsheets and scrubbing pots, she pulled the magazine out and locked it in a cabinet on the back porch. She put Irene in the old baby basket and set her on the living room floor and placed Junior on the area rug while she reorganized the desk. By the time George and Anna returned from school, she had moved the magazine three more times. She stood at the front window waiting for Walter. But he was late.

The vast majority of state institutions are dreary ... Death comes faster to the abused...

She sat down on the edge of the velvet chair. The sound of Junior shaking the Warrior can did not soothe her this evening, but instead, she listened to the clock, hearing each tick. At some point, something soft nudged her leg. It was Anna, tucking a teddy bear between the chair and her thigh.

The clock ticked louder.

She couldn't remember if this was one of the evenings for Walter's meetings. Junior was not going to be put in the pantry, at least not until Walter got home. Instead, she covered him with a blanket, keeping him on the living room floor by her feet. She watched his every move. How his legs curled up and hugged his body. How his head tucked into his chest and how he sucked his thumb. Her eyes only left his figure when car lights appeared on the road. She didn't even turn on a lamp as the room eventually went dark. Her eyelids were heavy. The velvet chair offered little comfort. She nudged opened the front window. Cold air seeped into the room. A car roared in the distance, its headlights emerging larger, only to quickly pass her house.

The victim ... screamed in agony ... George was killed here, 1937...

Her eyes fixed on the second floor. Her gnawed fingertips began to hurt. She looked at Junior and Irene. Another car drove by. Her body melted into the chair. Her head dropped.

She was above a group of people dressed in white. They were stacked in a pile, forming a strange heap. They seemed to be crying, but she couldn't hear them. An arm poked out from underneath the bodies. It was bony and waving to an invisible orchestra. She tried to move, but couldn't. She pushed harder, but her body was lead. Her mouth opened to scream, but nothing came out. The door to the room slowly opened. A large attendant appeared. He had a set of restraints in his hands. He began searching the pile, calling her name. Then she felt the touch of his hand on her arm.

"Ruth?"

She opened her eyes and was looking at Walter.

A loose thread from his parent's bedspread was twisted between George's fingers. "But Ma," he said, "she's always telling us we're doing something wrong." He sat on the bed next to his mother, his legs bouncing.

"I know," she replied. "But she needs help setting up the picnic."

His mother was removing bobby pins from his sister's hair. He watched as she filled a little jar with the brown clips.

"Why can't Eddie and Minnie help?" Anna asked.

"Because," she replied.

"But why do we need to go?" his sister added.

"Because she and Dziadzia are getting older and can't do the things they used to do."

George looked at his sister. Her uncombed hair made her look like medusa.

"It's scary over there," she said. "And I don't like the squirrel. It looks real."

He snuck his arm behind his sister's back and tapped her shoulder.

She jumped.

"Hold still," his mother said.

"But he tried to scare me," Anna replied.

His mother gave him a familiar look.

"What if she tries to give us a pile of clothes again?" he asked.

Anna's tight curls bounced in the opposite direction of his mother's brush. They were stubborn, like Anna.

"Well," his mother said, "just thank her."

"But some of the clothes had bugs in them," Anna said. "Remember?"

"I know. I'll sort through them again."

He continued to bounce his legs, skimming his toes along the floor. "She always says, 'You children need to dress like the rich.'" He thought his imitation of his grandmother was pretty good, accent and everything. It even made Anna smile.

"She just wants what's best for you," his mother said. "That's all."

His mother had a way of making his grandmother nicer than she really was.

"Are you coming later with Junior?" he asked.

"Yes."

"I thought Busia didn't like him there," Anna said.

"Well, there's no one to babysit him, so he's coming with me, your father, and Irene."

"It's like you have two babies," Anna said.

His mother let out a loud sigh.

Anna was always saying the wrong things.

"I hate when she says I need to be more ladylike," Anna added.

"You?" he said. "A lady?"

Anna crossed her arms and made a face at him.

He made a face back.

"Run upstairs and grab a bow," his mother said. She turned to him. "You be on your best behavior, young man."

He grinned—not an intentional grin—it just happened.

His mother stood up and moved to the closed pantry. He watched her press her ear against the wood. She squinted and slowly opened the door. He could see Junior, laying on his bed, in his usual position, his legs huddled to his chest and his eyes closed.

"Do you want to get up?" she asked.

He didn't know why his mother kept asking Junior questions. He wasn't going to answer but his eyes did flutter open.

She lowered the guard rail and moved him to a seated position. She knelt on the floor and peered under the bed. "George," she said. "His can. Grab it for me." Her fingers snapped at him, the kind of finger-snapping she does a lot.

He got down on his hands and knees and crawled into the small space. Even though it stunk in there, it was cleaner than under his bed. His fingers stretched and touched the can, but only pushed it farther away. He felt Junior's weight bouncing on the bed.

"Got it!" he said. His head thumped the bottom of the bed as he tried to get out.

Junior squealed.

George crawled backward, freeing himself from the cramped space.

His mother moved Junior out of the pantry.

"You're not going to dress him to match me. Are you?" he asked.

"Yes," she replied. "Of course. He's your brother."

"**A**nna!"

Anna looked at her grandparent's kitchen window. The bright summer sun temporarily blinded her, forcing her to salute the house.

"Yes, Busia?" she replied.

Her grandmother's face was in the window frame. She could've been any old lady, except her voice was distinguished and disturbing the peaceful day. "Come in here," she called.

Anna stood up. The picnic table had a checkered tablecloth on it and a few green leaves. They were pretty, but she brushed them off the table. George was standing next to their grandfather by the grill.

"Anna!" Her grandmother's voice boomed again.

She saw George look at her. His eyes narrowed and his face contorted into a scary look. She frowned at him and turned away. The backyard was covered with green grass, except for a few flowers. They were bright yellow and pretty. She snapped one of the stems and spun the flower between her fingers.

"Anna!" Her grandmother kept calling.

She skipped into the house and into the kitchen. It was a sharp contrast to her home, with spotless floors and a glass vase on the table. Hovering near the sink stood her grandmother. Steam billowed from a pot in the basin, making it look like she was breathing fire.

Anna leaned over the table toward the glass vase. She smiled at her reflection and stuck her tongue out. She placed her yellow flower into the vase.

"No," her grandmother said.

She jumped back.

"That's a dandelion. Throw it away." Her grandmother pointed to a waste basket.

Anna looked at the dandelion. She brought it to her nose, pretending it smelled like a rose.

Her grandmother's finger wagged under her face and pointed to the waste basket again.

She peeked inside the can. It was nearly empty. Egg shells and a chicken carcass sat on the bottom. She preferred to look at the dandelion. Twirling the stem, she tucked it behind her ear.

"It's a weed," her grandmother said.

"But I like it," she replied.

"Go get the candle from the coffee table in the front room," her grandmother said.

She didn't want to go into that room, but she didn't want to stay in the kitchen with her grandmother either.

"Go on," her grandmother said.

She walked into the dark room. Giant ogres of wooden furniture loomed tall, and shadows cast by flowered drapes exposed willowy insect legs that seemed to be waiting to catch her. She looked around the quiet space but avoided the front door. Her eyes scanned the chair with evil animal claws that pointed to the coffee table and the candle. It was sitting in a glass bowl the color of blood.

A creak sounded from inside the room. Her eyes flashed

toward the door. The glassy eyes of the stuffed squirrel stared at her, silent and screaming. She ran to the table and grabbed the candle. Then dashed from the room.

"Take it to the picnic table," her grandmother said. "And don't drop it."

She pushed the backdoor open, running into the outside world.

36

SPINNING GRENADE

George watched his aunt place a cake on the picnic table and straighten a wrinkle in the tablecloth. "Happy birthday, Pa," she said as she batted her eyelashes at her own cake.

"Thank you, Margie," his grandfather responded. His words sounded pleased but his tone was surprised.

"How's your mother, George?" his aunt asked.

He was sitting at one end of the table. His chin rested in his hands and his elbows splayed over the checkered cloth. No matter how far away he was from her, her nasal voice sounded like a flat horn.

"She's fine," he replied.

"Take your elbows off the table," she said.

Her spiderlike fingers whizzed past his eyes, flicking a leaf from the tablecloth. He wanted to stay seated and watch the charcoal briquettes get stacked into a pyramid, but he stood up and moved into the yard.

"Eddie," his aunt called. "Come sit down."

He eyed his cousin as he wandered over to his mother, like a dutiful fathead. His crisp white shirt and pleated shorts crinkled as he kicked his sister's rubber ball.

"Eddie got straight As in school this year," his aunt said. "How did you do?" She had a way of singing her words, and they always sounded off pitch.

"Good," he replied. He picked up the ball, tossed it above his head then caught it.

"Eddie, sit up straight," his aunt said.

His cousin pinched his shoulders back and straightened his neck, the side part of his slicked brown hair revealed a strip of shiny, pasty scalp.

"Eddie won the science award this year," she said. "Did you?"

"Margie." His grandfather's voice also sounded like a song, just a different kind.

"What?" she said. "I'm just asking."

"Ollie, you want one?" His uncle called from the opened garage. One of his hands held a refrigerator door open, the other held up a brown bottle.

"Already got one, Ed."

George heard a car turning into the driveway. His uncle's Plymouth Special De Luxe, parked close to the garage, made his father's used Hudson look like a jalopy. He ran to greet his parents.

The driver's door opened and his father stepped out. A long low whistle blew from his lips. "Ed," he called. "You must be gettin' pennies from heaven!"

George looked at his uncle, whose chest puffed forward as he walked to his car. His fingers slid over the chrome edging as the two men circled the shiny maroon sedan.

"This doll has a push button starter, dual windshield wipers, rear window vents," his uncle said.

His father whistled again.

"No choke to start 'er," his uncle continued. "Just turn the ignition key and she purrs like a kitten." His uncle's fingers glided over the hood. "Here, lemme show you," he added.

George watched him stroll over to the driver's door. He slid under the massive steering wheel, his body bouncing on the puffy seat. Sparkling gages and chrome glistened from the dashboard. He turned the key and a slow, easy whirl hummed from under the hood.

"Walter!" His mother called from the backseat of the Hudson.

His father nudged his arm. "Go help your mother," he said, his eyes fixed on the Plymouth's dashboard.

George ran to the car and opened the backdoor.

His mother was holding Irene on her lap and sitting next to Junior. His brother was wearing the same shirt and shorts as he was.

"Grab the pies for me," she said.

The sweet, familiar aroma of cinnamon led him to the front seat. He reached for one of the pie tins. It was warm. The golden crust made his mouth water.

"Take one at a time," she said.

"I can carry both." He dug his hands under each pie plate.

"Careful, George," she said.

"Ma, I'm okay." Wiggling the pie tins with his fingers, he carefully inched them to the center of his palms.

He saw Anna and Minnie, running down the sidewalk toward him. He lifted the pastry tins into the air, just in time. The girls rushed past him. Then he spotted Eddie swinging his leg over the picnic bench and slowly rolling the ball under his shoe. Eddie's foot pulled back, then sprung forward. The ball spun down the sidewalk, heading straight in George's direction. He steadied the pies and leaped over the spinning grenade. Eddie, the wise guy, was smiling and shrugging.

37

NO LONGER A LITTLE BOY

R uth heard Walter whistling at Ed's Plymouth on his way to the back of their car.

"Will you get the baby basket out?" she asked.

She watched as he opened the trunk. Inside was Junior's old baby basket along with a diaper bag. She placed Irene in the basket and put the bag on Walter's shoulder.

"Take her to the picnic table," she said. She walked to the side of the car and opened Junior's door. His legs were awkwardly bent, one close to his chest, the other splayed across the seat. She positioned each foot on the floorboard, then, one by one, swung each leg through the opened door. His feet landed clumsily on the driveway. Earlier when she dressed him, she put a pair of Walter's old shoes on his feet and, although they fit, they just didn't look right. She flattened each foot on the cement and pulled him closer to the door. Sliding one hand under his armpit and grabbing the roof of the car with the other, she pulled him forward.

"Come on," she said.

He grunted loudly. One of his arms swung outward, hitting the side of the door and causing him to yelp.

She placed her foot on the bottom of the door frame and tugged him upward. "Stand up," she said.

He stood up. He was almost her height. She patted a loose strand of his blonde hair into place and straightened his shirt collar and suspenders.

"This way," she said. She walked with him on the sidewalk, her arm tucked around his back.

"Hello, Margaret," she said. "Your dress is pretty."

Her sister's eyes were roving over Junior. "Hello, Ruth," she replied. "I thought you were leaving him home."

A carnivorous grunt escaped Junior's throat, fluctuating between boy and man.

"No, he's here with us," she said. "Where's Mother?"

"She's inside."

The backdoor screen bounced as she guided Junior into the house. The small mud room smelled familiar, but Junior's nose scrunched. She pulled his arm, encouraging him to move, but he unexpectedly stopped. "Come on," she whispered.

Despite her repeated tugs, he did not move.

"Junior," she said. "Come on."

He grunted then began to walk. His bony knees and legs poked out from underneath his shorts, each step exaggerated, like a baby deer.

Inside the kitchen, the sun beamed through the windows, but the room was flooded with artificial light. Anna and Minnie were standing near a paper sack and shucking corn. Her mother was next to the girls and pointing at the sack.

"Hello, Mother," she said.

"I thought you were leaving him home," her mother replied.

"You know I can't find a babysitter."

She watched her mother's foot nudging the paper sack directly under the girls' hands.

"Is he going to behave?" her mother asked.

"He'll do the best he can," she replied. She didn't look at her mother, but was watching Anna examine the bright yellow corncob.

"I hope you brought extra diapers for him," her mother said, picking at Anna's corncob and rotated it in her hand.

"Yes, of course, I did. Do you need help with anything?"

Her mother shoved the corncob back into Anna's hands and pointed to clingy silk strands. "Everything's almost ready," she said.

Ruth watched her daughter's fingers rub and flick at the corn threads. Junior let out a tiny chirp. She looked at him. He was looking at the vase on the table. She looked at the vase too. His reflection looked like Walter.

"You missed," her mother said.

Ruth turned toward the girls. Loose green husks were on the floor next to the bag. Her mother's shoulders rolled back and her glasses slid down her nose. Ruth dropped Junior's arm and picked up the discarded husks.

The sudden sound of her mother's snapping fingers sent a chill across her neck.

"No!" her mother said.

Ruth looked up. Junior was walking toward the living room.

"No!" her mother said again.

He continued walking, his fingers sliding over the wall, leaving a trail of dirt. Her mother lurched toward him, but Ruth dropped the corn husk and reached Junior first.

"That boy is too much for you to handle," her mother said. "I told you, you should've left him at home."

"I can't find anyone to help me," Ruth said. "You know that." As much as she tried to steady her voice, it still wavered.

"I don't understand you," her mother said. "Just place him in the asylum and be done with it."

Ruth looked at the two girls. Anna was frowning at her grandmother.

"You read that article, just like I did," she said, pulling Junior to the sink.

"Take him to the bathroom," her mother said. "I don't want a mess in here."

The kitchen sink looked blurry as she stared at the faucet. She could feel Anna standing right behind her. Moving away from her mother, she led Junior into the bathroom. The small room was warm. She turned the faucet on and looked into the mirror. Junior was no longer a little boy. His neck was thick, like a man's, his eyebrows seemed to be bushier and his ears stuck out, almost perpendicular to this head. His eyes fluttered, then suddenly, he looked directly at her.

"Junior?" she whispered. She wanted him to answer. She wanted to hear his voice. She wanted him to say he was fine and everything was going to be okay. But instead, he grunted and pulled his hands away from the faucet.

38

The willow tree by the picnic table rustled in the summer breeze. Ruth looked at the shape of branches she knew so well. As a child, she loved to sit under the tree and read. Back then, she didn't have a care in the world. It was just her and her books, and Margaret rarely sat in the backyard.

"It's nice how you dress Junior and George alike," Margaret said, plopping a scoop of potato salad on her son's plate.

"Ma," Eddie said, "I can serve myself. I'm not an imbecile."

Ruth looked at her sister. She was smirking. "Of course you're not," she replied. "Mother, pass the cucumbers."

Junior's plate was in front of Ruth. A small pile of square-cut onions and crescent-shaped celery pieces filled a portion of the dish. She smashed potato salad into a paste. Her free hand was resting on Junior's arms, pressing them into his lap.

"Stop it, George!" Anna yelled.

She looked at a small table in the yard shared by Anna

and Minnie. Minnie was poking a spoon at her doll's cupid mouth and Anna was aiming her spoon at George.

"What's going on?" Ruth asked.

"He threw a cherry at me," Anna said.

"You see Hutchinson throw that ball?" Ed was talking to her father and Walter.

"What a pitch!" her father said.

She spooned the mashed potatoes into Junior's gaping mouth. A grunt gurgled from his throat and it was loud. She could feel everyone staring at her. "Junior," she said with a smile, "it's okay." She rubbed his hands. They were wiggling, but she kept them settled on his lap.

"Sure was a good game," Walter said.

She was about to feed Junior another scoop, when a stream of gooey potatoes dribbled from his mouth. She scraped the spoon over his chin and wiggled it between his lips.

"Yeah, tonight's game should be another——" Ed's words halted.

Runny potatoes were oozing from Junior's mouth and his eyes were clamped shut. His body lurched forward in spasmodic waves and suddenly, undigested food violently flew in all directions. Everyone tilted backward and Eddie's hands flew up in the air as pieces of clumpy white stuff covered his shirt.

"Ruth!" Margaret's face puckered like a needle being pushed into a pin cushion. "We're eating. Can't you feed him later?"

Her efforts to tame Junior's unsettled body were lost. His hands banged the table with fury. Despite the thick tablecloth, silverware and glasses rattled across the wooden planks, and Junior's grunts bubbled out, louder than before. She looked at Walter. He was looking down at his plate.

Pulling Junior to a standing position, she dodged his punching arms as he screamed and yelped.

"George," she called. "Find his can."

She wrapped her arms around Junior and struggled to control his turbulent limbs. His feet pounded and scraped over the grass as she dragged him near the house. Sweat trickled down her forehead as she pushed him to be seated. But he resisted.

A moment later, George was by her side with the can of marbles.

"Place them on the ground," she murmured.

He put the can on the grass. Junior's grunts and howls became louder. His clenched fists swung wildly, missing her dodging head.

"Rattle it a little," she hurriedly whispered.

George bent down and rattled the can.

Junior's head turned. He plopped down on the grass.

"Eeewww, what's that smell?" Minnie cried.

Junior dug his hands down his pants.

"Ruth!" Margaret said. "Control him, please!"

She pulled at Junior, trying to lift him off the ground, but his twelve year old body felt like the weight of a car. She circled her arms under one of his armpits, pulling and tugging, but only lifting him an inch off the ground. A hand appeared from behind her, slipping around Junior's back. She turned to thank George, but found herself looking at her mother.

PART IV

1950

Those who danced were thought to be quite insane
by those who could not hear the music.
— ANNE LOUISE GERMAINE DE STAËL-HOLSTEIN

39

AGAINST THE STREET

George passed the neighborhood grocery store. A soda pop ad was posted in the front window. His mouth watered. Sipping a pop sure would make writing his boring history report a bit easier. He liked reading about the presidents and the Indians, and stuff like that. But the women of the revolutionary war? That was boring. Very boring. Why did he need to know about how they kept the household or how the Daughters of Liberty was formed? Another left turn and his house was a block away. He could run, but he wasn't in a rush.

He heard laughter and it was getting louder. He turned the corner. A group of boys on their bikes were circling in the street, their words reaching his ears.

"Hey dummy, can't you talk?"

"What are you tryin' to say, ya moron?"

The tallest boy stopped his bike and let go of his handle bars. His arms turned mockingly inward and his wrists flexed oddly. "You give me the heebie-jeebies. Make that sound again, go on!"

The other boys laughed and howled.

George spotted Junior, wandering off the front porch and walking toward the group.

"Hey imbecile, come over here," the leader said. His body stiffened, like Frankenstein, moaning and grunting.

Adrenaline shot through George's veins. His walk became a trot. Then a run. "Leave him alone!" he yelled. He was closing the gap.

The leader looked his way and jumped off his bike. Metal clanked against the street.

"Junior!" George shouted. "Back to the house!"

Junior continued walking forward.

The leader planted his feet and hunched into a boxer's pose. His fists circled in the air and he was looking directly at George. The other boys had stopped their bikes, but they didn't get off.

"Hey, Frankenstein! Coming home to see your monster?" The words of the leader hit George like a punch.

George's speed was at full throttle. With only a few yards away, his right arm cocked back.

The leader threw a warning punch into the air.

George sprung forward, thrusting his fist into the leader's face, knocking him backward and flat on the street. He hovered over him, his bloody fist ready for another punch.

The leader blinked but didn't get up.

"Want another knuckle sandwich?" George asked, barely breathing enough air.

The leader crawled backward from underneath him.

"*George!*" The unmistakable voice of his mother was coming from the house.

He looked in her direction.

Her hands were wringing in her apron and she was running across the yard.

"What's going on?" she asked.

His arm lowered.

The leader stood up and ran.

"That's what I thought," George yelled to the disappearing boys.

"George! What on earth," she said. "Junior! How did you get outside?"

R uth sat at the table, plate untouched, and stared at the wall.

"Is this meatloaf cooked?"

The voice sounded familiar, but the words seemed distant and muffled.

When did those dirty fingerprints get on the wallpaper? She would clean them tomorrow. The voice started again. Faint, deadened words that bounced off her ears, as if she were underwater at the swimming pool. *Was she near a pool?*

"Ma?"

A different voice.

"Ma!"

She shook her head and looked around the table. Her eyes landed on George.

"Are you okay?" he asked.

She heard clicking.

"Ruth?" Walter was snapping his fingers at her. "Is this cooked?" he asked. His fork was in the air and he was pointing it at her. She looked at the pink meat dangling from the tines. It had a bright red center, like an unhealed wound.

She thought back on her day. The morning began as it

usually did, breakfast for everyone. Walter left for work and George and Anna went to school. She was sorting the laundry on the back porch. Days of clothes or maybe weeks, she wasn't sure. She was picking through Junior's dirty diapers, deciding which ones need extra cleaning when she heard a crash. She ran to investigate. Junior was in the kitchen standing among broken pieces of porcelain and cookies. She thought she had locked the pantry door. Irene was picking up cookie bits and sticking them in her mouth. Ruth had shooed her out of the room and started to clean the floor when she heard the front screen door bang shut. She ran through the living room to the front porch and found Junior outside, walking toward the street. She pulled him back into the house and locked him in the pantry, then went back into the kitchen, where Irene was screaming with a bloody foot.

That's when the telephone rang. It was the school nurse. Anna was sick and needed to be picked up. She bandaged Irene's foot and told her to find her shoes, went into the living room to get Junior, but he wasn't there. She ran out the front door and looked down the sidewalk. She ran back into the house, through the living room, into the kitchen, and into the back porch. He was nowhere. She ran up the stairs, searching the rooms and almost tripped on the steps running down. That was the moment she heard the can of marbles rattling in the pantry. She opened the locked door and saw Junior sitting on his bed. She touched him to make sure he was real. She rushed him to the living room and put Irene's shoes on. In Walter's workshop, she pulled the wagon out and placed Irene inside, and she rushed down the street pulling Junior with one hand and the wagon with the other.

The classroom doors were closed and the hallways were empty, so she followed the signs to the nurse's office when she smelled something foul. Junior had his hands down his pants and she didn't bring his diaper bag. Outside the nurse's door, she pushed him into a seated position and knocked on the unlatched door, pushing it open. Anna was sitting in a chair with her head bowed and a stack of books on her lap. The nurse motioned for her to come in, but she remained in the doorway, next to Junior.

Back at home, she was mixing ground beef and an egg when Anna yelled from the living room. Shoving the meatloaf into the oven, she ran to investigate. Junior was sitting on the velvet chair, his hands full of feces. She had forgotten to change him when they got home. She yanked his arm, trying to lift him, but he was fighting her and wouldn't budge. His dirty fingers were grabbing at her face as she wrestled him, but she couldn't maneuver the sixteen-year-old out of the chair. Anna stood behind him, pushing at his back and Irene pulled at his leg. She finally got him to the bathroom and into the tub. She striped off his clothes, which revealed a hardened penis. She ordered the girls out of the room.

"I think I forgot to turn the oven back on," she said.

41

CONVULSING

Thumping and banging noises woke Ruth from a fitful sleep. For a moment, the senseless sounds were baffling. Then she was fully aware. Leaping out of the bed, she frantically fought with the lock on the pantry door and opened it. Junior was lying on his bed, covered in feces. A sheet was tangled around his neck and arms and his body was convulsing.

42

DANGEROUS

W alter drove the Hudson through the parking lot of the Toledo Asylum for the Insane. The jostling of the pitted pavement added to the tremor in Ruth's voice.

"She didn't even ask his name," she said.

He glanced at his wife. Tears bordered the rims of her eyes. Her nose looked rosy and cold as she dabbed a crumpled handkerchief at her face.

"And why couldn't we see the cottages?" she asked.

Her hand gripped the window crank, budging the window open. Cold October air seeped inside. He watched her eyelashes flicker, dropping a teardrop onto the burgundy booklet in her lap. He gripped the gear lever and pushed the clutch to the floorboard. The sudden jolt shifted their bodies like a hiccup.

"I don't think this is a good idea," she continued.

He thought of the past year. The way she had changed. She was quieter, withdrawn. She barely slept. Her hands trembled and there was a slight hunch to her back. Her beautiful chestnut eyes, once full of happiness, now looked sad. Terribly sad.

He cleared his voice. "You heard what the clerk said," he began. "The cottage system. It's a good system. Better than the big ole asylum buildings. And it's run by doctors and nurses that are trained to deal with people like him. He'll be in one of those. And an attendant will be by his side, night and day."

He glanced at her as she unbuttoned her coat collar. The wool fabric loosened from her neck, but her thin fingers wrapped her throat, causing him to wonder if she was getting sick. He shifted the gear knob, rumbling the Hudson along Detroit Avenue.

"He's better off with me," she said.

"No," he said. The single word thrust from his throat. He emphasized it with a shake of his head. "That's the best place for him. And it'll be good for you too." He thumped the dashboard's oil pressure needle causing it to flicker. "Besides," he added, "you can visit him almost every day."

"She didn't ask even one question about him."

Her breath looked like steam, puffing from a locomotive and circling each dangerous word.

"This isn't a good idea," she said.

Despite the slow speed of the car, he thought the houses were blurring past. "This is the right decision," he said. "When we get home, I'll fill out the paperwork and you read that book." He pointed to the tear stained burgundy booklet: *Mental illness; a guide for the family.*

In the bedroom Ruth gripped the curtain cord. It felt cold and heavy. A canopy of thick dust covered the oak dresser under the window. She felt a teardrop rolling down her cheek, but didn't stop it. Instead she let it fall, disturbing the dust on an old bowl of lavender sachets. Slowly, she opened the golden drapes and looked outside. Turbulent clouds hung in the sky, like an unstable demon.

She turned to the room. Dressed in his Sunday finest was Junior, sitting on her bed. His bony fingers wrapped the Warrior can. A murmured hum remained stranded in his throat. She picked up Walter's Brylcreem tube and removed the cap. Stiff, lifeless paste oozed onto her palm as she looked at her son.

His eyes fluttered.

She laced strands of his blonde hair between her fingers, thickening his feathery hair with each caress.

The wooden floorboards creaked. She saw George tiptoeing into the room and he was carrying Walter's shoeshine box. He knelt on the floor and picked up one of Junior's scuffed shoes. She touched his arm. He looked up at her, his eyes looked scared.

She knelt next to him and removed the shoe from his hand.

Without a word, he stood up and left her alone with Junior.

44

UNDERWATER

A row of bumps and divots rocked the Hudson, shaking Ruth and Junior in the backseat. She squeezed Junior's gloved hand and moved closer to him. The seat was ice cold, piercing through her wool coat as if she were still in her nightgown. Between rugged potholes, she fastened the top button of his coat. His elbow swung upward and jabbed her in the ribs. She caught his arm and placed it back at his side. Her hand rested on his glove, rubbing his fingers as if the movement would stop her tears. Her body shivered, like the oil pressure needle underneath Walter's tapping finger. The ten-minute drive to the asylum seemed like one long breath. Underwater. Like when she was a young girl, swimming in Lake Erie, looking through murky brown water, watching her feet sink into the soft muddy bottom. The hermetic lake would take her to another world, driving her soul into the center of her body. Her name bubbled through the water, becoming clearer and clearer.

"Ruth?"

Walter's eyes peered at her in the rearview mirror.

"We're here," he announced.

She heard the engine sputter off. The door opened, then closed. She heard Walter's footsteps clicking on the surface of the parking lot. The back door opened. His outstretched palm beckoned to her like a ghostly spirit. The seat turned colder as she slid closer to the door but her hand remained attached to Junior. She moved his gangly legs out of the Hudson. His shoes clicked against the pavement, like Walter's.

"No," she said. "This is wrong."

She could feel her body falling, but Walter's arm wouldn't let her hit the ground.

"They will take care of him," he whispered. "I promise."

She wanted to grasp his words, place them in her pocket, but they disappeared.

45

BLOODSHOT

The registration waiting room was crowded. Walter scanned the space. Tightly linked chairs stuffed the room and almost every seat was taken. An assortment of mismatched folding chairs were crammed against the wall, creating walkways as crooked as the cracks on the ceiling.

Walter looked at Ruth. She looked scared.

"Find a seat," he said. "I'll let them know we're here."

The line leading to the registration window snaked along the only wall without chairs. He stood at the back of the line, watching Ruth and Junior zigzag through a warped maze. She was leading him to the only empty seats by a window. People gawked at his son who shuffled through a cluttered aisle, his deep grunts rising above the murmured voices of the room.

He turned away from those faces and examined the wall. Dirty crown molding and cracked baroque tiles gave an illusion of past elegance. He thought about ways he could add putty to the cracks and make it look new. He preferred to think about that.

The man in front of him turned to the woman next to

him, probably his wife. He was showing her the same burgundy brochure Ruth had at the house. His finger was aimed at a photograph of a smiling doctor. She stared at the image and placed her hand on the boy in front of her.

Walter tapped the man on the back. "Excuse me," he said.

The man twisted his head toward Walter but kept his body facing forward.

"Are you checking your son in here too?" Walter asked. The words caught in his throat.

The man nodded then turned back to his family.

Walter looked back into the room. Despite the cold October day, the dark space was humid and reeking of beer and onions. A Victrola console was pushed into a corner and the swinging sound of clarinets and saxophones floated in the air. He could easily have been in a lodge or union hall. But he wasn't.

He reached inside his coat pocket and pulled out a thick envelope. He stared at the words on the cover. Toledo Asylum for the Insane. He looked around the room again. The gawking faces had changed to frowns and they were twitching and humming and talking. He couldn't tell the new patients from the family members. He looked toward the window, searching for his wife and son. They were sitting and she was pulling Junior's coat tighter around his neck. Her eyes looked sad, even from across the room. He jabbed the envelope at his sweaty palm, packing it down like a deck of Luckies. The line shuffled forward. The man in front of Walter took a breath so deep Walter thought he might burst into song.

Instead he heard a scream.

He turned toward the noise and so did the jittery crowd. An old lady had her arms around a young girl who was sobbing. Walter looked at Ruth. She was watching the young girl too.

The family in front of Walter shuffled to the registration window.

He heard the woman's voice. "Will my son be okay?" she asked. She was leaning toward the screen window. It was grainy and distorting the room behind it.

He looked back at Ruth. Her hand was hovering over the windowsill, searching along the casing and her purse was on the ledge, blocking what appeared to be a draft. Junior was sitting in his chair, his head bobbing from side to side, his arms conducting his silent orchestra. Something pecked at Walter's shoulder.

"You're next," a voice from behind him said.

Walter stepped to the screen.

"Can I help you?" the clerk asked. Her voice sounded annoyed and her eyes were not looking at him, instead she was shuffling through paperwork on the counter.

The closer his face got to the gritty screen, the clearer the office behind it became. The bright overhead lights flooded the protected room, highlighting stacks of files piled on three desks. Cabinet drawers, opened at different lengths, had papers sticking out and keeping the drawers from closing properly. A portly nurse was rummaging through an opened drawer, her back hunched like a squirrel. There were only two people in the office and he thought no matter how hard they worked, there would always be a pile of papers taller than them.

His forehead bumped the screen. A strong smell of bleach burned his nose. He cleared his throat.

The clerk looked up.

"Can I help you?" she said again. Her rigid white collar peeked out from a blue suit that magnified her bloodshot eyes.

His mouth was dry. "Well," he began. "My son—"

"We want to see your institution." Ruth's voice was loud and in his ear and she was standing right next to him.

He looked at her. Her nose was almost touching the screen.

"Ma'am, what is the nature of your problem?" the clerk asked, her voice was flat but surprised.

"Oh, it's not for me, it's for our son," Ruth replied.

Walter looked at the clerk.

"Uh huh," she said. Her annoyed voice was back. She opened the screen window and slid a burgundy brochure toward Ruth. "Here's some information to read," she added.

He reached for the brochure, but Ruth pushed it back. "We already have this," she said. "We want to see your cottages."

The clerk's eyes seemed to dull, as if she were about to fall asleep.

"Our institution is closed to the public. We accept patients that have broken minds, hereditary dispositions, epileptic fits, asthma, mental diseases, people who need time away, the feeble minded, imbeciles and idiots." She seemed to be reciting a memorized script like prayer in church.

"What about the article in *Life Magazine*?" Ruth's blunt words surprised him.

The clerk paused before continuing her canned dialog. "We offer hydrotherapy, elaborate diets, social hour, and baseball. And we've cured many patients and sent them home to their families."

"And the article?" Ruth repeated. Her finger tips were pressed against the screen. Walter was certain the clerk could see fleshy little pink pillows from her side.

The clerk stopped and stared at Ruth, then she looked at him.

The portly nurse ambled to the window. "Oh, you know how magazines are," she said. "They write gossip, anything to make some sugar."

Her words were dismissing and she did not impress Walter.

"Along with our cottages, we have an auditorium, a greenhouse and farm, lagoons, dining hall and, of course, a chapel," the clerk said. She aimed the brochure toward Walter.

He didn't reach for it.

"Come back when you're ready," the portly nurse added, wandering back to her files.

"But our son," he said. "He's already been accepted. You're supposed to be expecting him."

"Oh," the clerk said. "Name?"

46

MISTER

"Janikowski?"

Ruth shifted in her chair and looked across the waiting room to a nurse standing in a doorway. Her fleshy backside was holding the door open leading to a long tunnel on the other side.

"Mr. Walter Janikowski Junior?" the nurse said, emphasizing *mister*, as if she were singing the name of a dignitary.

Ruth saw the people in the waiting room search the crowd. She looked around the room too, but didn't stand up. She knew Walter was staring at her but she didn't look at him.

"That's us," he said, nudging her arm.

She saw him stand up. He was pulling Junior from the chair. She clutched at Junior's arm, pulling him back into the seat, but he was already standing upright.

"Come on," Walter said.

She stood up and grabbed Junior's arm, Walter held the other. She couldn't remember the last time she saw Walter touching Junior. He started to lead Junior away from her. She held onto his arm, but he was still walking away. Junior's was wobbling through outstretched feet cluttering the crooked aisles.

She stared at the floor. The waiting room tile abruptly ended under the nurse's clean white shoes.

"Janikowski?" the nurse asked.

"Yes," Walter replied.

The nurse led them into the hallway. Walter went first, pulling Junior. Ruth stepped behind them. A black and white checkered floor twisted her vision with a hallucination of an endless tunnel. Her shoes temporarily stuck to the floor with each step.

"We have a high recovery rate for those afflicted with the manic depressives, dementia types, and schizophrenia," the nurse said.

Ruth looked at the walls. They were covered with thick beige paint that clashed with the black and white tiled floor. Faint yellow lights dotted the walls, but it seemed dark.

She stared at Junior's feet. His toes turned inward, his shoes slapped the floor with clumsy thuds. The clickity clack of the nurse's gait echoed in her ears.

"Someone will be in shortly," the nurse said, opening the door to an examining room.

47

The doctor's white smock was immaculate, clashing with a grimy examining room. Ruth looked around the space. The lower half of the walls were covered with tiles, and although they were white, they were soiled and cracked. Skinny, black electrical piping stemmed from the ceiling, and Ruth felt as if they were standing under a sinister daddy longlegs. She spotted a pile of debris in a corner and strained to analyze its contents.

"My wife can no longer care for him."

She winced at Walter's words as she watched the doctor circling Junior, scrutinizing his body as if he were inspecting a special cut of meat.

"He has convulsions," Walter added.

"I understand," the doctor said.

She stared at the man. He was looking in Junior's ear as if this were a routine visit.

"My wife has to do everything for him. He wears a diaper. And has to be fed."

"Soft food only," she said. "And a bottle."

The doctor lifted Junior's chin toward the ceiling causing his eyes to flutter in the bright light.

Junior grunted.

She recognized this particular grunt. It was one of resistance, but the doctor's forceful palm held his skull at an unusual angle.

Junior's arms flung upward, hitting the man in the face and nearly knocking off his glasses.

"We'll take care of him," the doctor said.

Her vision turned watery, but she was watching the man's every move: the way he adjusted his glasses, the way he picked up a pen and a clipboard. He seemed to be an average man, not a doctor.

"Here's his bag with his clothes," Walter said.

"I can bring more if you need me to," she added.

"That won't be necessary."

The scratching sound of the doctor's pen on the clipboard echoed in her ears, becoming louder with each second. She dug her fingernails into the palms of her hands.

"And," she said, "I brought his favorite toy," she choked out the words. A tear rolled down her cheek as she held the Warrior can of marbles. Its label was worn and faded, but the fierce Indian profile was still visible. Junior grunted with the rattles. "Please don't let him be without it," she added.

"I understand," the doctor replied.

The scratching was even louder than before.

"How does this process work?" Walter asked.

"Well, he will first reside in the admissions ward where preliminary examinations are made. Then we will determine which cottage he will be placed in and what treatments are needed."

"What do you mean by treatments?" she asked, glaring at the doctor.

"That will be determined once we establish your son's physical and psychological status," he said.

She didn't like the way he was rustling the clipboard pages and the way he wouldn't meet her stare.

"He won't be harmed, will he?" she asked.

The doctor peered over the top of his glasses and looked directly at her.

"Dr. Frazer," Walter interjected, "what my wife means is she wants to make sure he is receiving the best of care."

The doctor put his pen down. "Mrs. Janikowski, we study people like your son. We know how to care for them. He'll do just fine." The scratching on the clipboard started again.

She looked at Walter. He was nodding at the doctor.

"The nurse said you have a high recovery rate and some patients get to go home. Will he come home?" she asked.

The doctor looked at the examining table. Junior's mouth hung open. His head swayed.

"Ma'am, we'll do what we can," he said.

"When can I come visit?" she asked.

"The patient first needs to acclimate to the institution for thirty days before family can visit. You can get the details from the clerk," he said opening the door. "Someone will be in shortly to take your son to receiving."

She stared at the door. It was closing slowly.

"Walter," she whispered. "Let's get him outta here." She rushed to Junior and pushed his arm through one of his coat sleeves.

"Ruth, you heard what the doctor said. They will give him the best treatment—"

"I didn't hear him say, 'the best treatment,' " she said. "You said, 'best treatment.' He only said, 'treatment' not 'the best treatment.' " She ran to the other side of the table, pulling the coat over Junior's shoulders. "This is a mistake," she said. "Just look at this filthy—"

The door flung open. Two large attendants dressed in white charged in.

She felt Walter's hands pulling her away from Junior.

The attendants surrounded her son and grabbed him.

Junior screamed, flailing his arms and legs wildly.

"No! Let him go!" she yelled. She yanked her arms, but Walter's grip was strong.

Within a moment, the men lifted Junior into the air and had him on a gurney in the hall. She finally wrestled free from Walter and ran after Junior. The two attendants were tightening large straps over his squirming body. Junior was screaming and swatting at their brawny hands, like an animal fighting for his life.

"What are you doing?" she yelled. "He's a harmless boy!" She was pulling at one of the straps, trying to undo the buckle when she heard footsteps running down the hall. Walter grabbed her arms and pulled her away. She watched as Dr. Frazer rolled up Junior's sleeve and plunged a needle in his arm. Clear liquid disappeared from the syringe into his skinny limb. Within a moment, Junior was limp.

"Ma'am," the doctor said, "this is just a procedure. Your boy will get the care he needs."

48

THE VELVET CHAIR

Walter leaned against the kitchen doorway watching Ruth. She had been sitting in the velvet chair for hours, staring out the living room window. The first few weeks without Junior, she wandered around the house, from room to room. A few times, he found her sitting on the front porch with an empty pot on her lap. Other times he found her staring at the telephone. But most of the time, he found her sitting in the pantry, crying into one of Junior's T-shirts. Walter reminded her the first visiting day was this Thursday. Her shoulders straightened, and for a moment, he thought there was joy in her eyes. But he wasn't sure.

W alter stood behind his chair in the kitchen, his hands resting on the top rail as he watched Ruth. She was standing at the stove and wearing a dress she would normally wear to church, but it was a Tuesday.

She grabbed an egg from a bowl and held it above a frying pan. "Scrambled or over easy?" she asked.

"Over easy," he replied.

He watched her tap the egg against the skillet, her wrist flicking as if she were casting a spell. The sound of sizzling filled the room.

"Everything's ready," she said.

He eyed the imaginary line from her spatula to Junior's chair. Ruth's brother's military field bag rested in the seat.

"I've got a blanket, an extra pair of pants, the picture Irene drew, and applesauce," she said.

He knew that rucksack once held weapons, but now, he wasn't sure what it really contained.

"And I've decided on *Curious George* instead of *Pinocchio*."

He pulled out his chair, careful not to scrape it against the floor, and sat down. His eyes didn't leave his wife as he watched her tip the pan, letting the egg slide out onto a waiting plate.

"I think *Curious George* will be better," she said. "He might even be able to follow along now. Besides, I read him *Pinocchio* before he left."

He scanned the bag again. A sharp object poked at the canvas pocket, causing him to wonder if his wife had hidden a knife.

"Irene's going next door, and George and Anna are going with me," she said.

He looked at the full plate in front of him. Next to it was his newspaper. He didn't need to go outside and find it this morning. Instead it was waiting for him.

50

A TEST

Anna watched her mother fold the corners of a napkin around a spoon. Silverware was not usually allowed in the living room, but today was a special day.

"Where's Irene?" George asked.

"She's next door," her mother replied.

Anna ran to the side window. The neighbor's house was on the other side of the driveway. She squinted at their double windows, but a reflection of gray sky was all she could see.

"Why do we have to leave so early?" George said. "The Snake Pit's not that far away."

Anna turned to her mother, waiting for George to get *the look*, but instead, her mother's long fingers rolled the cloth into something that resembled a flimsy cabbage roll.

"We don't want to be late," her mother said. "And don't call it that."

She watched her brother slide his foot into a boot and stomp across the floor. It reminded her of his terrible dancing.

"I love being out of school," she said. "We were supposed to have a test today."

"I know," her mother replied. "I spoke to your teacher. You'll have to take the test tomorrow. And don't forget your gloves."

Anna thought of her schoolmates, their pencils wiggling the answers, as she skipped around the living room. Her dancing was better than George's.

The harsh ring of the telephone upset the room. Her mother rushed to the stairs. "Hello?" she said. Loud muffled words buzzed from the receiver. "I can't talk now, Mother. It's the first visiting day, remember?"

Anna watched her mother hang up the telephone, nearly knocking over the little stand.

"You just hung up on Busia," George said.

Anna started skipping again.

51

BARREN

The old man sharing a bus seat with George plucked a grape from a brown sack. Ruth was sitting behind them, watching as the man rolled the small purple fruit between his fingers, holding it up to the window. His swollen knuckles matched the plumpness of the translucent orb as he inspected it like a jeweler. She glanced at Anna, sitting by her side. She was watching him too.

The bus slowed, then stopped. The driver leaned forward. Ruth watched as he turned his head one way, then the other. His big eyes appeared in the rear view mirror, darting back and forth, before looking directly at her. She quickly looked outside. The Detroit and Nebraska street signs were stacked one on top of each other. She focused on them.

The bus lurched ahead, pushing her forward, then, pressing her against the seat.

She felt a tap on her leg. It was Anna. She was pointing to the old man in front of her. He was popping a grape in his mouth and humming. George was inching his body closer to the edge of the seat. Ruth spotted his leg swinging into the aisle. Another intersection passed. Detroit and

South. She clutched the field bag on her lap. The worn canvas offered little comfort as she anticipated the next stop.

The driver looped his fingers around a gear lever. She watched as he nudged the skinny stick into another gear. "Next stop, Detroit and Arlington," he announced. "The insane asylum." His eyes were back in the rear view mirror. The bus lurched again, then slowed.

"This is our stop," she whispered.

Anna looked up at her. She looked frightened.

"It's okay," she said, "We're gonna see Junior."

The bus navigated to the side of the road. The sound of the brakes hissed as the bus came to a halt.

George stood up, blocking her view of the driver. He already had his hat on and was walking down the aisle before the bus doors squeaked open. The stuffed bag hit her back as she stood up and slung it over her shoulder. "Go in front of me," she said.

Anna slid out of the seat and into the aisle.

She felt the driver's eyes watching her every move until she was off the bus.

Freezing November air chilled her lungs and a heavy gray blanket hovered in the sky. A hot gust of air blew as the bus departed, sending a whiff of exhaust to her nose.

"Where is it?" George asked.

"It's down this sidewalk, behind the trees." She pointed to a barren patch of woods. A grand sidewalk gently arched around a group of leafless maples, shielding the street from the insane asylum grounds. Her gloved hands rested on the backs of her children and nudged them forward.

"The sky looks scary," Anna said, her voice low and quiet.

The meandering sidewalk curved around a big parking lot filled with cars. The same parking lot where she had been with Junior.

"This place is busy," Anna said.

"Is that it?" George was pointing to an opulent building nestled in a row of colossal structures from a bygone era.

"Yes," she replied.

"It looks like a castle," Anna said.

52

MISSION STATEMENT

Gothic buildings formed an oblong ring that surrounded the interior grounds of the insane asylum. The gruesome structures were close together and packed in a dense row.

Ruth pointed to the administrative building. "This is it," she said. It was in the center of the row, a formidable lord protecting a gluttonous king.

"How many buildings are here?" Anna asked.

"I'm not sure," she replied.

The threatening gray clouds darkened the mysterious entrance as she shuffled up the front steps. She looked at George and Anna. They were motionless and waiting on the sidewalk. "Come on," she said.

Inside the entrance parlor, elaborate woodwork surrounded each doorway and an oriental rug covered the floor. Her heels sunk into the plush rug as she looked around the room.

"Where's Junior?" Anna whispered.

Despite the full parking lot, the administrative building appeared empty and silent.

"I don't know, we have to find the visitor room first," she

said. A golden plaque hanging on the wall caught her eye. It read, "Mission Statement. To many the subject of caring for the insane is . . . a mystery. The secret of their care and keeping them contented is to have them lead as normal a life as possible, with good clean, healthy surroundings, plenty of nourishing food, and fresh air."

"This way," George said.

She looked at her son. He was standing next to a sign with an arrow. It was pointing to a dim hallway.

Titled golden plaques were anchored on each hall door.

Trustees' Parlor

Library

Telephone Office

Her eyes landed on a sign for the visitor's room. She twisted the door handle and walked inside. The room could have easily been the waiting room with the same tall ceiling, baroque tiles and screened window, except the chairs were in orderly rows and the room was completely empty.

"Who are you here to see?"

She looked toward the screened window. The beady eyes of a male clerk were eyeing her suspiciously.

"Well?" he asked.

"We're here to see Walter Janikowski Junior," she replied.

His elbows rested on the counter and he was tapping a pen against the screen frame.

"I guess we're the first ones to arrive." She didn't mean for her statement to sound like a question, but it did. A question he ignored.

"Name again?" he asked.

She moved closer to the screen. The smell of cigarettes and coffee was strong.

"Janikowski with a J," she replied.

He picked up an oversized leather book and dropped it on the counter with a bang. Opening the cover, he licked his finger. Each page was stained, either with a coffee ring or cigarette burn. Musky paper rustled by her face, sending a damp scent into the room. He turned page after page until his palm pressed down on a sheet of paper marked with a giant *J*. His finger slither down the list of names.

"Ah," he said, "Wilbur Janikowski, Cottage Six."

"Walter, not Wilbur," she said.

"Walter, that's what I said." His lips puckered up as he pushed a cigarette in his mouth.

"Ma," George whispered.

She looked at George. He was leaning toward a group of framed photographs hanging on the wall.

"This is when the asylum was first built," he said. "They had a baseball diamond."

"This pass is for one month," the clerk said. He slid a piece of paper through a small opening.

"Excuse me," she said, "My son's name is Walter, not Wilbur."

He slammed the leather book closed.

"Yes, I know," he said. "That's what it says."

"No, it says Wilbur." She pressed the piece of paper to the screen.

"Lady, don't matter. Cottage Six. Out the door to the left." His fish lips circled the cigarette, sucking the tobacco as if it were the last bit of air.

She pointed at her children. "Do they need a pass?"

"Nah," he said. His words were as rotten as his breath.

53

The backdoor of the administrative building swung open, hitting the wall with a clank. The wind whipped Ruth's hair against her face as she stepped outside and looked at the desolate field before her. A large oval ring of asylum buildings surrounded the frozen land, stretching over several acres. The field was covered with dead, frozen weeds flattened by a blanket of frost. The eerily quiet grounds seemed almost sacred.

She looked at her children. They were scanning the area too. "Come on," she said.

"Which way?" Anna asked.

The back of the asylum buildings mirrored the front, stately but battered. Pushing into the headwind, she leaned forward. "To the left," she answered. The frozen sidewalk made their footsteps echo through an amassment of brick and stone. The heavy field bag bounced against her back as she shifted the sack from one shoulder to the other.

"Want me to carry that?" George asked.

"No, I've got it," she said. "Let's move quickly."

The plummeting temperatures helped quicken her pace

as she ignored the sound of the wind snapping branches, like dead brittle bones.

"There's the chapel," Anna said. She was pointing to a structure with colorful stained glass windows. Ruth thought of Junior, sitting in a pew with an attendant, gazing at the vivid prisms and hearing joyful songs.

"Look for Cottage Six," she said.

A row of ghostly trees formed a macabre fence between sidewalk and road.

"Where are all the people?" George asked.

"Just keep going," she answered.

"Cottage One," Anna said.

Ruth looked at a tarnished golden plaque hanging on the front porch of the cottage. The letters were scratched and damaged, but they were still readable.

"And that one says Cottage Two," George said.

The two story cottages were made of dark brick and looked like houses, but they were ragged and unkempt. Ruth thought it could have been an ordinary neighborhood filled with ordinary people, except there was an air of superiority emanating from each building.

"Come on," she said. She looked ahead at the next cottage. At the top of the porch steps was an empty wheelchair with a bundle of cloth on its seat. Movement from an attic window caught her attention.

"What was that?" Anna whispered.

"I don't know," she answered. She grabbed Anna's hand.

The empty road led in a straight line, only to give way to a curve in the distance. The opposite side of the road opened into the expansive field and there was the empty baseball diamond.

"Ma, you're hurting my hand," Anna said.

Her grip loosened but she didn't let go. The wind howled and swirled between the cottages.

"There's some people," George said.

Ruth looked at Cottage Four. Two people were sitting on a porch swing. She waved to them, but they didn't move. She waved again. They still didn't move. The closer they got to Cottage Four, the clearer the two people became. They were giant bags of laundry.

"Ma? Is anyone here?" Anna asked.

"They're probably inside," she said.

The door to Cottage Five opened. A large man wearing a white uniform appeared in the entrance. He casually leaned against the door with his leg bent. His eyes locked on Ruth.

She forced a smile.

He struck a match on the doorframe, cupped his hands, and lit a cigarette.

She nodded to him.

Flinging his head back, he stared at her, then Anna.

Her grip tightened around her daughter's hand.

"Ma?" George asked, "Where's Cottage Six?"

The sidewalk banked sharply to the right forming a corner of the rectangular grounds. Two buildings, different from the cottages, edged the curve of the road.

"Library?" Anna questioned.

A small brick building was tucked into the outside corner of the curve, dwarfed by a humungous structure sitting next to it.

"And that one says *Infirm Ward*," George said, pointing to the mammoth building.

Ruth looked at the stone building ahead of them. It soared upward with asymmetrical architecture of irregularly shaped rooflines and parapets. The welcoming storybook-style windows and swirly structural design softly called to her. She abruptly stopped, yanking Anna's arm as she did. She looked back at Cottage Five. The attendant was still watching them. Then she turned to the Infirm Ward.

"Let's ask in there," she said.

The fancy exterior door looked like an old lady wearing cheap cosmetics. Lacy white curtains veiled the side windows of the carved wooden door with a mock cozy image. Notched in the chiseled framework was a silver doorbell. Under the pressure of her gloved finger, the small round button released an electrical buzz that vibrated inside. She leaned toward one of the windows. A fray in the closed curtains exposed shadowy stairs. The wintery daylight vaguely illuminated the first few steps. Stained feet with long curly nails were the only thing she could see.

She turned the door handle. It was locked.

A moment later, the dark entry was saturated with light and the seated man was visible. He was wearing ripped pajamas and a book was balanced on his head. His hands flew to his eyes, but the book remained steady. Bounding down the stairs was an attendant dressed in white like the man from Cottage Five. As he passed the seated man, he kicked him with the only dark item on his body other than his belt. The book fell off.

Ruth lurched backward, grabbing George and Anna.

The door cracked open. The attendant's scowling, puckered face poked through the narrow gap. "What is it?" he demanded.

"Excuse us," she said, "Where is Cottage Six?"

He shook his head in disgust. "To your right," he said and slammed the door shut.

"Come on," she said.

Across the street, the wind blew frozen bits of paper across the field, making it difficult to believe the baseball diamond once heard the crack of a bat.

"There," she said, pointing to the back of the asylum grounds. The road curved again and mirrored the opposite side of the field, dotted with identical brick cottages like the ones they just passed. In a moment they were in front of the first cottage. Clinging to a rotten porch column was the damaged sign of Cottage Six. Warped floorboards and peeling paint issued a warning she quickly dismissed.

High recovery rates for those afflicted. Some patients get to go home.

She rushed to the front door. Her raised fist ready to knock, but she paused. Foreign words, sung in operetta, punctured the cracked walls and spilled out onto the cold porch. She leaned into the door. The baritone's deep, hypnotic notes fluctuated into a string of unknown poetry, imitating the songs from her father's Victrola. The beautiful voice swayed in tone, but abruptly halted as she knocked on the door. Slithering metal rattled in the lock. She stepped away from the door, blocking George and Anna. The door swung open to reveal a hulking attendant, jangling a ring of keys. His once-white uniform was tinged with blotches the color of burned biscuits.

"Yea?" he said. His thick eyebrows pinched together, shadowing his dark eyes.

"We're here to visit my son," she said.

His clumsy elephantine fingers fumbled with the set of keys too small for his hands. He repeatedly struck the keyring against a metal loop on his belt, like a machine at a factory, until it caught. His enormous body swiveled in the doorway, suggesting a small tunnel and testing her will. Stepping in the narrow pathway, she stopped in front of the attendant allowing George and Anna to pass through. His hot breath moistened the back of her head, the smell of cigarettes circled her nose.

George and Anna entered the building but stopped in front of her. The stench of decaying cheese and stagnant water hung in the air, thick as an overflowing outhouse. There was no entry hall or boundary, it was just a large space. A dirty, dilapidated room filled with zombielike patients in bare feet and pajamas cluttering the ground, sitting and staring.

She pulled George and Anna close and turned to the attendant, but he was on the front porch, locking them inside.

A man sitting against the wall was wrapped in soiled linen, his arms strapped against his chest. Another was picking an opened wound on his foot and licking his fingers.

"Hello?" she called, searching for another attendant.

"Hello," came a response from the cluster of patients on the floor.

The hardwood planks creaked under their weight as they tiptoed through the room and into a cold hallway. A slice of dull light filtered into the hall from an open door.

"Hold Anna's other hand," she whispered to George as she led them to the room.

54

R usted cots, pushed side by side, filled every available space of the meager room. Each dirty mattress held more than one comatose body and the faces looked sedated and malnourished. Despite a cracked window, the cold room reeked of rotten eggs decomposing in sunlight.

Ruth stood in the doorway, searching the room. She handed the bag to George and whispered, "Wait right here." Her skin felt damp and cold as she tiptoed into a disjointed pathway.

In the back of the room, she spotted a bony arm, poking out from underneath a soiled sheet. Her pulse quickened. He was lying on his side, facing away from her. Squeezing between a lifeless hand and someone's foot, she pushed her way toward the back of the room. Junior was seconds away. She slithered sideways between rickety cots when cold, sticky fingers latched onto her hand, digging jagged nails into her palm. Choking a stifled gasp, she yanked her arm but the deathly grip would not release. She looked at the hand. It belonged to an old man. He was lying in a cot, his spindly legs curled to his chest and patches of oozing wounds covered his gray skin. He blinked at her. Dried mucus clung to the rims of his eyes, like desiccated glue pulling at sparse eyelashes. She touched his icy fingers. His grip released. She pulled a crumpled sheet over his body, tucking it under his emaciated limbs. His eyes closed.

She glanced at the doorway. George and Anna were huddled together, staring at her. Then she heard a quiet grunt. She searched for the bony arm. It was stretched in the air, touching the dingy wall.

"Junior?" she whispered. She inched her way closer to his cot. Standing at the edge of his bed, she touched his bony foot peeking out from the sheet.

The leg kicked.

"Leave me alone! Leave me alone!" A skinny young man sat up and yanked his body away from her. She fell backward, stumbling against a cot and a grabby hand. Regaining her balance, she quickly moved toward the door when something soft ran over her foot. She saw Anna's hand fly to her mouth, covering a silent scream as George mouthed the word *rat*, pointing under the cots.

55

MANGLED

George looked at his mother as she joined him and Anna in the hallway. She had a determined look on her face. He wanted to grab her and Anna and pull them out of the cottage and run, but he knew she wouldn't leave, not without seeing Junior first. His father taught him to notice the condition of buildings, the way they were built and the way they were kept up. He was sure this cottage hadn't been looked after in years, maybe even decades. The peeling wallpaper in the hallway exposed layers of plaster and the cracks in the floor were filled with unrecognizable things. It was not a place he wanted to be.

"Ma, where are the workers?" Anna whispered.

He was wondering the same thing. He watched his mother as she looked down the hallway, then her gaze focused on a staircase. She looked back at him and nodded.

He wanted to leave, but he also wanted to see Junior, so he nodded back.

A mesh lampshade covered a fixed light at the base of the stair rail. It looked damaged, like everything else, except the light was working and lit the bottom steps. The stairs lead straight up and the middle of each step looked lighter than the edges, as if someone had removed a stair runner. The wall opposite of the railing was gouged and scraped and covered with smeared fingerprints.

"Stay close," his mother whispered.

Each step had its own creak, creating a discord of wooden moans as they trudged upward. George felt the field bag on his shoulder suddenly shift. He turned around and saw a scruffy patient, whose mangled teeth were clamped onto a corner of the bag, his head was whipping back and forth like a dog.

George tried to pull the bag from the man. "Let go!" he yelled. Suddenly, an attendant materialized and pulled the man until his mouth went slack.

"Are you okay?" his mother asked him. Her eyes were wide and she looked scared.

He nodded, but he really wasn't sure.

"Please," she said to the attendant. "Where can I find my son?"

"Who's your son?"

"Walter Janikowski Junior," she replied.

"I dunno," he said. "Check upstairs."

George watched as the attendant disappeared down the hallway.

"Come on," his mother whispered.

They continued up the steps. He heard movement from the second floor.

A dominant voice said, "Take your medicine."

His mother began to run up the stairs. Anna was right behind her and he was behind Anna.

"Swallow it!" the voice boomed louder.

He heard a thud. They reached the second floor landing and an attendant was crouching over a teenage patient lying on the floor.

"Is everything okay?" his mother gasped.

The startled look on the attendant's face frightened

George. The man's eyes were glowing, like burning black coals.

"Where's my son?" His mother's voice was frantic, almost hysterical, but she was reaching toward the boy on the floor.

The attendant's muscular arm blocked her, almost touched her neck. "Ma'am," he said, "this is therapy."

George grabbed her arm. It was shaking.

"Where is my son?" she said.

"How do I know?"

"You work here," she said. "Now, where is he?" Each word she said seemed to be its own sentence.

"Maybe he's in there," the attendant replied.

George hated him. He felt fury as he watched the man smirking at his mother and pointing to a closed door with two deadbolts. The door was marked Violent Ward. The man's sly smile grew wider as he strummed a set of skeleton keys on his belt.

"Unlock it," his mother said.

George looked around the landing. It was sparse except for a chained file cabinet and the dazed patient sitting on the floor. Then he looked at the only window. It was covered with a chain-linked curtain and two nails were in the frame, blocking it from fully opening.

He heard the jingling of the attendant's key sliding into one of the deadbolts. "Have a look," he said. His amused tone was almost a laugh.

A woman's voice, gentle and calm, sailed into the space. He looked toward the stairs. "There, there," the kind voice said.

He looked at his mother. She was watching the staircase too.

A pretty, composed nurse stepped onto the landing. Her white uniform and thick stockings covered her body, revealing only a sliver of skin at her neck. "Hello," she said. Her rigid white cap bounced with her greeting.

"Thank heavens you're here," his mother said.

"What can I help you with?"

"I need to find my son."

"Okay," she said. "What's your son's name?"

"Walter Janikowski Junior," his mother replied.

The nurse slid her hand into her pocket and pulled out a set of keys that matched the attendant's. She unlocked the padlock on the file cabinet, letting it drop to the floor.

"Janikowski with a J?" she asked.

"Yes." George and his mother answered together.

The nurse put another key in the second cabinet drawer and pulled it open. He could hear her whispering their name over and over as her fingers touched each file.

The doorknob of the Violent Ward rattled. He looked at the attendant. He was smirking again and jiggling his keys.

"Here it is," the nurse said.

George eyed the file in her hand. It had a strange stain on the front. He watched as her eyes scanned the contents.

"He's in this room," she said, pointing to a white door.

George looked at the attendant.

He shrugged and laughed, locking the Violent Ward padlock.

56

T he nurse's wrist wiggled back and forth, jiggling the stubborn lock of Junior's room. Ruth stood by and waited. She wanted to grab the key and open it herself, but she didn't. A dirty worn patch around the doorknob made the faded white paint of the four-paneled door appear bright.

"We keep the lights off and the doors closed," the nurse said, "so they can sleep." Another flick of her wrist and the lock clicked. She gripped the porcelain doorknob but Ruth pushed the door open and walked inside.

Foul, pungent odors overpowered the nurse's flowery perfume causing a sharp pain in the back of Ruth's eyes. Like the room below, it was overcrowded with metal cots and sedated patients who churned at the movement from the door. She stepped deeper into the room. Thick, cold air swirled around her, touching her exposed neck.

She looked back at George and Anna standing in the doorway, their eyes fixed on her.

An urgent whimper traveled through the room.

She turned sideways and slid through a tiny gap between two cots. Gloomy daylight filtered through a chain-linked curtain attached to the only window in the room. A grunt broke through the silence. Her eyes targeted the sound. Next to the window sat Junior. He was strapped in a wheelchair.

Thrusting a path through the congested room, she shoved and rammed cots out of her way, scraping them over the floor and jostling patients awake.

She saw Junior's eyes flutter.

A few more feet and she could touch him.

Her arms stretched forward and her fingers grasped through the air. She pulled his body to hers. She inhaled his scent and pressed her cheek to his face. It was hollow and emaciated. Her eyes closed. Warm teardrops streak down her skin, dropping onto the back of his dirty pajamas. "Oh, Junior," she cried "I'm so sorry."

His thin hair brushed her eyelids, tangling with her damp lashes. Squeals and shrieks filled his throat.

"Let's get you out of here," she whispered.

Leather binds were attached to his wheelchair arms and legs, and to Junior. But his hands and feet were squirming underneath the bindings. Unbuckling the straps, she saw his skin, raw and scraped. His fists banged the wheelchair, rattling the metal, like his can of marbles.

"Where's your can?" she asked, looking around the room.

He grunted and kicked with her voice, his squeals high and quick.

Squatting down, she peered underneath the cots. Heaps of dirty clothes and pieces of rotting food cluttered the dark space.

"Ma'am?" A quiet voice murmured from a cot besides Junior.

She looked at the cot. A teenage boy wearing pajamas and two shirts was lying on his side. A bed sheet wrapped around his legs made him appear to be lying in a bag of bones.

"I think your son's toy is under that cot," he whispered.

She eyed the imaginary line coming from his finger. A wadded T-shirt clung to a cylindrical object in the shadow of the cot. Shuffling closer, her fingertips touched the sticky floor as her shoulder bumped the bedframe. She stretched and moved, reaching for the buried can but could not grab it. Junior's legs bounced against the wheelchair, rolling the contraption away from her. She grabbed the rotating wheel, changing its course and steadying it to a standstill.

"Stay here," she whispered, softly touching his leg.

She was about to crawl under the cot when the boy with the two shirts slid in front of her and underneath it. He pulled the can from the dirty cloth and wiped it against one of his shirts, then handed it to her.

"Thank you," she said. The boy nodded, his kind brown eyes glancing away from her gaze.

The marbles jingled and rattled, the room filled with Junior's squeals.

"What's going on in here?" the nurse asked.

Ruth charged over to the hall and asked, "Why is my son strapped in a wheelchair?"

"Which one of them is your son?" the nurse asked.

"Right there."

Junior sat in the wheelchair shaking his can of marbles.

"Well," the nurse said, "let me see."

Ruth followed her to the cabinet.

"What's the last name again?" the nurse asked.

"Janikowski," Ruth replied. "Second drawer."

As the nurse pulled the drawer open, Ruth glanced back into the room. Junior's wheelchair was wedged between two cots. She went back into his room and grabbed the wheelchair, pushing it through the crammed space and bulldozing a pathway to the door.

George and Anna stood motionless as she rolled the wheelchair onto the landing.

"When's the last time he was bathed?" she asked.

The nurse turned a few pages of the file. "He's in that chair because he might wander to the stairs without an attendant," she replied.

"And when's the last time he was bathed?" she repeated. His hair was greasy and slid between her fingers.

"The shift last night bathed all these patients," the nurse replied.

Ruth rubbed the back of Junior's neck. "No. He's not been bathed in a while," she said. "And I don't think any of those other patients have either."

"Well, the night shift is supposed to do that."

She noticed the nurse's tone. It changed from confident to quiet.

"And how often does his diaper get changed?" she asked.

The nurse didn't look at her but was stuffing the file back into the drawer.

"Nurse," she said. "Answer me."

"I don't know," the nurse said, her voice was now shaking. "I just started."

"When does he eat?" Ruth asked. "Do you feed him?"

"This is only my second day here," the nurse said. "The four o'clock shift, they'll do that."

"Do they know he can only eat soft food? And someone has to feed him?" Ruth felt her own voice getting louder, but the nurse didn't look at her. Instead, she appeared to be studying something in the top cabinet drawer.

"Nurse!" Ruth snapped. "Why aren't you answering my questions?"

The nurse finally looked at her. Her expression was blank and scared.

"Pull his record again," Ruth said, her voice was now low and quiet.

Shuffling through the second drawer, the nurse retrieved

the file again. "Well," she stuttered, "I'm sure they have all of that written right here."

"And his convulsions. Are they noted, too?"

The nurse was silent as she flipped through the pages.

Ruth approached the woman. "Can I see that?" she asked.

"No. It's for asylum personnel only."

Ruth reached for the file, but the nurse shoved it back into the drawer.

"And where are his things?"

"Ma'am. I'm sorry. I don't know."

Ruth opened the field bag on George's shoulder. She dug through its contents and pulled out a pair of Junior's trousers. She shook the pants out, then gathered the material of one of the legs and bunched it into a circle. Kneeling next to the wheelchair, she lifted one of Junior's cold feet.

"Ma'am, what are you doing?" the nurse asked.

She slid the condensed pant leg over his foot.

"Ma'am! What are you doing?" The nurse's voice sounded alarmed, but Ruth continued to inch the trousers over his pajamas and onto his knees. Junior's legs wobbled as she pulled him from the chair, shimmying the pants to his waist.

"Ma'am. Stop. You can't do that. I'll get in trouble. A doctor is the only one that can release a patient. You have to get permission first."

Ruth directed Anna to place the can of marbles in the bag. "He's coming with me," she said. "George, hand me the blanket."

She tucked Junior's pajamas into his pants and turned to the nurse. "Where are his shoes?" she asked.

"Ma'am. He cannot leave!"

Wrapping the blanket around Junior's shoulders, she

folded the corners underneath his collar. "He's not being cared for here," she said.

She heard the agitated patients stirring with the force of her words. The door to the Violent Ward swung open.

"What's going on out here?" the attendant asked.

"She's taking her son home," the nurse said.

Ruth watched the attendant from the side of her eyes and he was walking over to her.

"Ma'am," he said. "That patient has to stay here."

She looked at his massive size. Then she looked at her son, frail and weak. She scanned the landing. It was rickety and the only way out was the stairs.

"Well," she said, forcing a smile, "I'm just going to take him home."

"No," the attendant said and pointed to the wheelchair.

"But," she opened her palms to him, "this will make it easier for you."

He pointed to the wheelchair again.

"Wouldn't it be nice to have one less patient to worry about?" she asked.

His hands wrung in a circle, cracking his knuckles. "If you don't put him back in that room," he said. "I will."

She didn't like the way he was staring at her, as if he wanted her to try to take her son out of the building. She turned to Junior and moved his wheelchair behind his legs. His bony shoulders flinched as she gently pushed him into the rolling seat. Her eyes were filling with tears as she pushed him back into the room and rolled him to the window. The boy with the two shirts was watching her. She looked into his kind eyes and he shook his head. She made her way back to the landing and grabbed the bag from George.

"I'm going to feed him," she said and reentered the room. She twisted the cap of the applesauce jar and spooned the food into Junior's mouth. Each bite was met with eagerness and squeals until the applesauce was gone.

"Ma'am," the nurse called from the doorway. "Visiting hours are almost over."

Capping the empty jar, she shoved it back into the bag and pulled out a book. "Here," she said, handing it to the boy with the two shirts. "I know it's a child's book, but it's all I have with me."

His dirty hand reached for the bright yellow cartoon. For a moment, their hands shared the cold book cover.

"They don't allow us to have things like this in here," he whispered and let go.

She looked at *Curious George*. He was being pulled by two firemen, like a common criminal. "I'm going to tuck it under your mattress," she said.

"Ma!"

George was in the doorway, his voice a loud whisper. "Don't forget his can. It's in the bag."

She took the can of marbles out and placed it on Junior's lap. She squeezed his hands and put them over the can.

"I'll be back tomorrow and get you out of here," she whispered. "Just hang on."

57

MAKE AN APPOINTMENT

Ruth's palm pressed the screen of the registration window. "I want to see one of the doctors?" she said.

"Ma'am, we've already been through this. There aren't any available right now." The woman on the other side of the window was the same clerk that checked Junior in.

"But you told me I needed to get a doctor's authorization for my son's release."

"Yes, that's right."

"Well, then I need to see a doctor," Ruth said, "to have him sign the release form."

"Ma'am, I understand what you're saying. But you'll have to make an appointment."

"I did make an appointment," Ruth said, "but it's not until January. I want to see a doctor today."

She watched the clerk make an obvious gesture to look at the waiting line behind her before she replied. "They're not here. They're on rounds."

"What do you mean on rounds?" Ruth asked.

"They're checking on patients," the clerk said. "You know, what you've been asking about."

"So, you're saying there's not one doctor here, in this building?" Ruth stared at the clerk.

The clerk was staring back. "Ma'am, they might be in this building, but they're busy," she said. "I'm sorry, but that's all I can tell you."

"Come on, lady." An anxious voice from the line was talking to Ruth. She turned around to a cluster of stressed faces, all looking at her.

Sounds from the loud speaker scratched in the waiting room. The clearing of a throat could be heard, then the words. "Visiting hours have started."

With the previous day's memories fresh in her mind, the only thing stopping Ruth from running to Cottage Six was the icy sidewalk. This time she was at the asylum alone. Last night she told Walter about the visit and how bad Junior looked. She put sheets on Junior's bed in the pantry and said she was bringing him home, but from the way Walter looked at her, she knew he didn't fully believe what she was saying.

"How could he lose that much weight in one month?" he asked.

She tried to explain how the attendants didn't seem to know what they were doing and how the nurse had just started working there. And the other patients were skinny and neglected, too. But he kept talking about Dr. Edwards and how the man seemed convinced that the asylum was good.

Today her plan was different. As she walked through the asylum grounds, the field bag bounced against her side and despite the frigid November temperature, she was sweating. She passed Cottage Three and looked for the empty wheelchair. It was still there, near the porch steps, in the same exact spot as yesterday.

Her pace quickened. The door to Cottage Five banged open in the wind. A man with only a sheet tied around his waist bolted down the front porch steps. As he raced across her path, an unbearable stench filled her nose. One of his arms waved to the empty baseball diamond, the other gripped the unraveling sheet.

"Frankie!" he yelled. "*Frankie!*" His voice was hoarse and deep. Jumping over dead branches, he nearly slipped on the icy grounds as he headed toward the abandoned field.

"Get back here!"

Ruth looked at Cottage Five. Two attendants raced down the steps and charged right past her. She watched as the gap between the men began to close. The patient ran into the field, flinging himself onto the frozen dirt. The sheet untied, tangling in his legs. His outstretched arm reached for an invisible base as if an umpire was about to call him out. One of the attendants jumped on him, twisting his arms behind his back. The other began kicking his head. The man went limp but the attendant continued to kick until his shoe was splattered with bright red blood. Ruth could see, even at a distance, their thick chests heaving. Picking him up by his elbows, the attendants dragged him over the field like a heavy bag of baseball bats and the soiled sheet clung to his ankle, leaving a ghostly trail. He was pulled onto the sidewalk in front of her.

"Pardon, ma'am," one of the attendants said. He nodded to her, as if he was crossing a busy street.

The naked man looked up at her. Veins throbbed on his forehead and blood was smeared over his nose and mouth. "Where's Frankie?" he whispered.

Ruth began to run.

On the porch of Cottage Six lay an upside down wheelchair.

59

IT DIDN'T MATTER

F lakes of paint flew in the air as Ruth pummeled the front door of Junior's cottage. She only ceased the barrage to lean toward the door and listen for an answer. Faint muffled voices could be heard, but the words were not distinguishable. She banged on the door again. "Hello?" she called.

No answer.

She pushed the overturned wheelchair out of her way. One of its wheels spun a whirl of clicking noises that slowly came to a stop. She stepped over a broken floor plank on the porch and stood in front of a window. A smeared circle of mud covered the wavy glass pane but she could see closed curtains on the inside. She stood back and surveyed the front porch. Almost every piece of siding and floor board looked rotten. Placing her hands on the splintered window frame, she jiggled it, but it was painted shut. Then, the front door clicked and opened.

A thin-faced attendant was looking at her. His forehead wrinkled as he asked, "Whadda ya want?"

"I'm coming in," she said.

His lip bulged and moved as he spit a filthy wad of saliva on the steps.

"Get outta my way," she said and pushed past him.

The same stench from yesterday was still in the main room, along with the same comatose patients.

"Is there a doctor in the building?" she asked.

"Naw," he said.

She stepped over the legs of a sleeping man as she moved through the room.

"Move it," the attendant said to the man. "Lady in the house."

She weaved around the patients, making her way to the staircase. The lampshade was missing from the stair light, exposing a puddle of urine on the bottom step and milky mucus on the handrail. She was halfway to the second floor when a hand clutched her ankle and pulled her leg. She grabbed the sticky railing and stopped herself from sliding down the steps. Then she looked at the hand. A man with thick eyebrows was squeezing her ankle, the same man from yesterday that tried to grab the bag from George. He was snarling a deep, low snarl, exposing yellow decaying teeth. She flexed her leg, connecting a sharp kick with his nose. His head jerked backward as he released her foot and tumbled against the stair rail, then down the steps. She scrambled for balance before prying her fingers from the sticky handrail. Clasping the bag to her chest, she looked at the man. He was curled up at the bottom of the steps. She quickly clawed her way to a standing position and moved upward.

The man sprung up and hurdled up the stairs two at a time, like a wolf. She raced to the top, but his teeth latched on to a corner of her coat, causing her to lurch backward and grab the handrail again. She steadied herself and looked at him. His clenched jaw moved back and forth, tugging at the material. She pulled at her coat and the fabric began to tear. Suddenly, his mouth went slack, causing her to fall up the stairs and him down. He grinned at her, showing a bleeding mouth with a missing tooth. She looked at the wet corner of her coat. A yellow, bloody tooth was sticking out of the fabric. Flicking the material, the tooth ricocheted off the wall. She turned and rushed up the stairs, grabbing the top rail and swinging herself onto the second floor landing.

The sound of rustling paper abruptly stopped. Stooped over the opened file cabinet was an old nurse pushing her slumped body upright. Her thick white stockings covered her bulging knees and skinny calves.

"Excuse me," Ruth said, trying to catch her breath.

The nurse turned around. "What are you doing up here?"

"I'm going in that room," she replied, crossing the landing.

"You can't just go in there," the nurse said.

"Yes, I can. It's visiting hours and I can see my son." She turned the doorknob, but it was locked.

"Like I said," the nurse repeated, "You can't just go in there."

Ruth looked at the woman. She had a long, thin nose and a streak of white hair that made her look like a skunk. "You need to open this door," she said.

"Who are you here to visit?"

"My son. Walter Janikowski Junior."

"And do you have a visitor's pass?"

"Right here." Ruth pulled out the pass from her pocket and waved it in front of the nurse's long nose.

The nurse grabbed it out of her hand. "It says Wilbur. Wilbur Janikowski, not Walter."

Ruth pulled it away. "The clerk told me it didn't matter," she said. "Now open this door."

"Okay, fine," the nurse said. She slid a key into Junior's door.

Ruth adjusted the heavy bag on her shoulder, the applesauce jar hit her sharply in the back. The door opened, she covered her nose and mouth and walked into the room. A shriveled old man was sitting in Junior's wheelchair by the window. She pushed her way through the tight space, fighting to get to the chair. The old man's head wobbled as her hand landed on the handle.

"Junior?" she called to the room.

"Yes?" A man replied from inside the space.

She turned to the voice.

A toothless man was laying on a cot, looking at her. She looked away.

"Junior?" she said again.

"Right here," the toothless man replied. This time he was waving at her.

She turned away a second time, then looked at the cot next to the wheelchair. The patient's legs were huddled to his chest and he was wearing two shirts.

She tapped his leg. "Excuse me," she whispered.

His foot recoiled from her fingers.

"Do you know where my son is?"

The young man rolled over. He rubbed his eyes and slowly sat up.

"Remember me from yesterday?" she said. "I'm Junior's mother, the boy that was in the wheelchair. Do you know where he is?"

He shook his head. "I haven't seen him since last night," he whispered.

"What?"

The young man shrugged.

She raced to the landing. "Where's my son?"

The nurse's scrawny finger covered her wrinkled lips as she hissed. "Lower your voice."

"Where's my son?" she repeated.

"What patient are you talking about?" the nurse asked.

Ruth ran to the Violent Ward and pulled at the door. "Where is my son?" she screamed. She looked at the nurse then ran to the file cabinet and opened the second drawer.

"You can't do that!" the nurse yelled.

She was pulling out files when the nurse's hands grabbed her arm and pulled it away from the drawer. One of the files flew up in the air and landed on the floor.

"Stop!" the nurse yelled.

Ruth slapped the skinny hands away from her and returned to the drawer.

The nurse grabbed her arm again, tugging and pulling, but she yanked free, causing the woman to stumble backward.

"I'm gonna get a doctor!" the nurse yelled, rushing to the stairs.

"Yes," Ruth said. "Get a doctor!"

Files flicked underneath her moving fingers, flashing partial names, until she landed on one with the letters *Janiko*.

60

Paper-clipped to the inside cover of Junior's file was a black and white photograph. Ruth stared at the image of Junior. He was wearing the same shirt and suspenders she dressed him in on the day he was admitted. His sunken eyes must have fluttered as the camera snapped, making his face distorted and ghostly, but the sweetness and innocence was still there. She grasped the edge of the picture, careful not to touch the printed middle, and wiggled it loose from its clasp. She held the image to her chest and closed her eyes. "Where are you?" she whispered. Then she slid it back into place and looked at the first page.

The admissions report listed Junior's vital information. His age, height, weight, blood pressure, temperature, and other details scribbled in pen, the handwriting rushed and sometimes illegible.

She scanned the page until she spotted the section outlining the reasons for admissions.

1. Severe mental deficiency (mental age of an infant)
2. Cerebral palsy; spastic type; involvement most severe in the lower extremities.

The scribbling continued in the note section with words of *acute mental retardation, idiot imbecile, epileptic affliction,* and *limited motor skills.* At the bottom of the page, a scribbled line read: *Mother brought toy.*

She flipped through the pages. Behavior report, dietary requirements, therapy/medicine. The pages were almost all blank and there was no mention of where he had been moved.

The Violent Ward door suddenly swung open. She watched as the same, massive attendant from yesterday walked out of the room and spotted her. "What are you doing?" he asked.

She slowly closed the file as he started to walk over to her.

"I said, what are you doing?" he repeated.

Without taking her eyes off him, she inched the file into the stuffed drawer.

The weight of his body pounded the floorboards as he stepped closer to her.

"Lady," he said, his voice low and quiet, "What are you doing?"

She ran to the stairs and spotted the wolfman sitting on the bottom step. She pounded down the steps and pushed past him, leaping onto the first floor before he had a chance to grab her. She ran into the main room. "Open the door!" she yelled.

The thin-faced attendant was leaning against the door, packing tobacco in his cheek.

"Open the door," she repeated.

His forehead pinched, but he didn't move.

She reached for his arm and pushed him aside. Grabbing the doorknob, she twisted and jiggled it, but it was locked.

"What's goin' on?" he asked.

"Open this door. Now!"

He fumbled with his keys, but quickly opened the door.

She ran onto the porch and into the freezing wind, passed the overturned wheelchair, but her heel caught on something and she fell down the steps, landing on her hands and knees. The field bag crashed on the sidewalk next to her.

She heard a distant voice. "Ma'am! Are you okay?"

The frozen sidewalk dulled the pain, but when she leaned back and looked at her palms, they were scraped bright red with tiny bits of gravel stuck to them.

"Ma'am," the voice called again.

A gloved hand appeared in her vision. She looked up. A guard, bundled in a thick coat, was standing over her with his hand extended.

"Are you okay?" he asked.

She looked at the bag lying next to her. It had a wet mark seeping through it and Junior's pants and a knit cap were scattered in the yard.

"I got a call," he said.

She took his hand. He pulled her upright.

"Are you okay?" he repeated. His face looked worried.

"I think so," she said. She picked up the bag. Chunks of applesauce and a piece of glass fell onto the sidewalk.

"Is there some sort of trouble here?" he asked.

"I can't find my son," she answered.

He was holding Junior's pants and cap. "What do you mean?" he asked.

"He's missing and I can't find him."

"Where is he supposed to be?"

"There," she said, pointing to the cottage behind her.

She saw him look past her.

"In Cottage Six?" he asked.

"Yes, but he's not in there."

A metal box was hanging from his shoulder. She eyed the telephone handset attached to it and a ring of keys clutched in his hand. They looked identical to the ones the attendants had.

"Did you ask the nurse?" he asked.

"Yes, but she left."

"What do you mean she left?"

"She left to get a doctor," she said, "but she hasn't come back."

She saw him scanning the deserted grounds. The glacial winds whipped through the trees; the sway of their branches was the only movement. His shoulders were flexed upward, pushing his scarf to his ears, then his gaze was back on her face.

"Did you look in every room?" he asked.

"No," she said. "I don't have keys."

She looked at the key ring in his hand, then up to his face. Out of the corner of her eye, she saw him slowly put the keys into his pocket, his gaze remained fixed on her. She glanced at his pocket, then his face.

He fidgeted. "No, ma'am. I cannot go in there," he said. "Not without a doctor's order."

61

ONLY ONE NURSE

Ruth walked the guard inside the cottage and pointed to the stairs.

"Is he supposed to be up there?" he whispered. Despite his bulky size, she thought his voice sounded small.

She led him past the wolfman and up the stairs.

"Where are the attendants?" the guard asked.

"I don't know," she replied.

The second floor landing was alive with activity. A patient was at the window, chipping at the frame with a pen. Another was sitting on the floor, shuffling through a file. Another was searching through a cabinet drawer, pulling files out, then shoving them back in.

"Where's a nurse?" the guard asked.

The patients' heads turned in his direction. She watched their eyes rove over his uniform, his nightstick, and the metal box at his side. They glanced at one another but didn't stop what they were doing.

"As far as I can tell," she said. "There's only one nurse."

"Only one nurse?" he asked. "What about the attendants?"

She shrugged.

"My son is supposed to be in this room," she said. The door to Junior's room was wide open and she walked inside. She was about to say something to the guard but when she turned around, he was still in the doorway, his hand covering his nose.

She pushed her way into the room. Most of the patients were awake, including the boy with two shirts. "Has my son come back yet?" she asked.

"No," he said.

She looked at the guard. He was watching her. She made her way back to the landing, stepping into a stream of flying woodchips.

"Hey!" The guard's voice was sharp and clear.

The patient stopped chopping.

"Get back to your room," he said.

She watched as the patient stared at the guard, sizing him up.

"I said, get back to your room," the guard repeated. This time, his voice was low and quiet and his hand was resting on his nightstick.

The patient laughed and tucked the pen into his pajamas then walked back into Junior's room.

"Can you go in that room with me?" she asked. Her hand was shaking as she pointed to the Violent Ward door.

"Ma'am, I'm not even supposed to be in here," he answered.

62

L ight from the landing trickled into the darkened space of the Violent Ward. Ruth heard what sounded like a pack of animals breathing in unison, their heavy breaths stirring up a stench of spoiled meat. She waited by the door as the guard scanned the room with his flashlight. A circle of light roamed the side of the room then stopped. She heard a click. Bright lights flickered on. She looked at the disturbing scene before her. Wooden school desks, bolted one behind the other, formed tight rows, optimizing the crammed space. Patients in straightjackets were sitting in each desk, their canvas-strapped arms and harnessed legs forced into freakish positions. Large buckets sat under each seat catching droppings of urine and feces. Every patient was slumped over, their heads inside empty bowls.

She covered her nose and mouth as she scanned the room looking for an odd-shaped skull.

"Is he in here?" the guard whispered.

"No," she responded and tiptoed out of the space.

"It smells terrible," he said.

His place by the door couldn't block the stench coming

from the room. She slid past him. He closed the door and turned his head, as if he received an invisible slap.

The stagnant air of the landing replaced the putrid smell of the room. She waited as the guard locked the door.

"I want to know," he whispered. "Who's caring for these people?"

She wanted to throw up. From the look on his face, he did too.

The hanging metal box on his shoulder buzzed. He picked up the receiver, holding it to his face like a regular telephone. "Kasprzak here," he said. His voice snapped into command with the inaudible words from the receiver. Then he hung up the handset.

"I've got to go," he said.

"But my son," she replied. "I still don't know where he is."

"I'm sorry, but they're calling me."

She watched as he tested the Violent Ward lock. She scanned the landing, spotting a thin door in a corner.

"Can you unlock this door before you leave?" she asked.

63

A LITTLE LAMB

The nearly hidden panel door silently opened. Inside, a narrow staircase led upward in the dark. Ruth placed her hands against the frosty walls and her foot on the first step. As she moved higher, the air became colder and harsher. Voices from the landing drifted into the staircase. She looked below. An arm pulled the door shut, darkening the already darkened passageway. Dust swirled from the moving door, forcing her eyelids to blink rapidly. She continued upward. Outdoor light trickled onto the top step. Above, a childlike voice was humming what sounded like "Mary Had a Little Lamb." The field bag slipped from her shoulder, pulling her coat away from her neck. The top button popped off and clinked down the steps. The humming stopped. She stepped onto the attic floor. Frost blanketed portions of the A-framed space, and in the middle of the sparse room was an armchair with a patient sitting in it. Lumps of pink flesh crowded his eye sockets, destroying the possibility of any sight. Thick, stained blankets wrapped his body but revealed swollen fingers gripping the ends of the chair arms.

"Is someone there?" His voice was as sweet as a child's.

She looked around the undersized room. Stacks of dishes were piled in a corner with bits of frozen food scattered on the floor. A bucket, like the ones from the Violent Ward, was near the opened window and a broken pair of glasses was hanging from a ceiling cord.

"Hello?" he said.

She stumbled for a response.

The man started to whimper.

She stood motionless, unsure of what to do.

His body started to shake.

"I'm not going to hurt you," she whispered.

The man began to scream. His shrill tone pierced her ears in a pitch that could break glass.

She ran toward the stairs and pounded down each step until she was at the bottom. She wiggled the doorknob and opened it.

"What were you doing up there?" A young nurse was standing on the opposite side of the hidden door.

Ruth stared at her.

"Well?" The nurse's eyes were twitching back and forth, like the second hand of a broken clock.

"I'm trying to find my son," she responded, sick of explaining herself.

"Where is he supposed to be?"

"In that room," she said. "And why doesn't anybody know where he is?"

The woman's eyes widened but she didn't ask any more questions. Instead, she reached in her uniform pocket and pulled out a ring of keys.

Ruth grabbed the keys from her hand.

"Hey!" the nurse said. "You can't do that."

"Which key is it?"

"I'm supposed to do that," she said.

"Are you new?"

The nurse nodded.

Ruth stuck different keys into the lock until she found the right one. She scanned the familiar faces but did not see Junior.

"He's not in here!" she said. "Where's the other nurse?"

"There wasn't anyone here when I got here."

Ruth looked at her. "Were you here yesterday?" she asked.

"Yes," the nurse answered.

"What shift did you work?"

"The evening shift," the nurse replied. "It was my first day."

"He was here yesterday. Was he moved somewhere last night?"

"I don't know who you're talking about."

Ruth went to the file cabinet and pulled out the second drawer.

"Ma'am, you can't do that."

Yanking Junior's file out, she waved the black and white photograph at the nurse. "Do you recognize him?" she asked.

She waited for the nurse's answer, thrusting the photograph in the woman's face.

"*Do you recognize him?*" she asked again.

She watched as the young woman leaned back and looked at the picture. "Oh dear," she said. "I think that's the boy who was sleeping under the cots."

Ruth threw the file at her and rushed into the room. She knelt on the floor, scanning the balled up sheets under the cots. She called Junior's name. Slinking lower, she crawled deeper under the beds until she spotted a bony foot. She heard a grunt.

"Junior?" Tugging a sheet free from his body, he appeared.

Brown streaks covered his face and pajamas, and the clip from his bulky diaper was sticking to his head.

"Oh, Junior," she cried.

"Ma'am?" the nurse called. "Where are you?"

She emerged from under the cots with Junior.

64

Brown water spurted from the bathroom faucet of Cottage Six. Two lidless toilets and a mildew-covered tub surrounded the rusted sink. Ruth watched the water change from brown, to orange, to yellow. And as the flow became stronger, patches of thick, grimy sludge flaked loose from the basin, splashing onto her wool coat. A small towel from her bag morphed from dry to wet as she held it under the stream, dropping chunks of applesauce into the sink.

Junior grunted. She looked at him. His bare foot was rubbing the slimy floor. A stuck cigarette butt rolled free from the bottom of his foot.

"Where are the towels in this place?" She called to the nurse.

She wiped the applesauce doused rag over Junior's grimy fingers.

"Nurse?" she called again.

The young woman came rushing in.

"Where are the towels?" she repeated.

"I'm sorry, I don't know."

"Can you help me look?"

She stared at the nurse. Smudged makeup around her watery eyes made her look like a frightened child.

"I'll see if one of the attendants downstairs knows where they are," the nurse said, then disappeared from the room.

Ruth dabbed the cloth over Junior's eyes but the caked on dirt wouldn't budge. She rubbed harder. He grunted and winced, pulling away from her.

"Oh Junior," she whispered. "Don't worry. I'm getting you outta here today."

His head bobbled and swayed when she spoke to him.

"Where is that nurse?" she hissed. Looking toward the doorway, a silver knob caught her eye as the nurse stepped back into the room.

"Did you find a towel?" Ruth asked.

The nurse shook her head.

"Did you find an attendant?"

The nurse shook her head again.

"When you were here last night," Ruth asked, "what did you use?"

"It was my first day," she said. "They only brought me here to see where I was gonna work. I was only in this building about an hour. The rest of my shift was filling out paperwork in the administrative building."

Her thick clumpy eyelashes quivered as she looked at the floor.

"What's that cabinet for?" Ruth said, pointing to the silver knob.

The young woman jiggled the locked handle.

"Use your keys," Ruth said.

"I can't find them." The nurse's quiet voice trailed off as she patted the pockets of her uniform.

"Watch him," Ruth said.

Crossing the landing, she passed through flying wood chips. The patient with the pen was back at the windowsill. She looked at Junior's door and spotted a ring

214 | VICTORIA ARENDT

of keys hanging from it. She wiggled the key loose from the lock.

"Get back to your room!" The sound of the nurse's voice was loud.

Ruth looked toward the window. The nurse was shaking her finger at the patient. Ruth slipped the key ring into her pocket.

"I said, get back to your room," the nurse repeated.

The patient stood up. He stared at the nurse then swung his arm, striking her in the head.

A quick, short scream left her throat as she fell to the floor. The man hovered over her, yelling about missing cigarettes and spitting on her face. She screamed and yelled as Ruth pulled at his arm, but he yanked it away and lunged at the nurse's throat.

Heavy footsteps pounded up the stairs.

An attendant rounded the corner, grabbing the man and tackling him to the floor. The man's chest was pressed into the floorboard as the attendant's knee pushed at his back. He pulled out a set of restraints from his pocket, and cuffed the man like a criminal. The nurse was leaning to one side, pushing herself up. Ruth grabbed her arm and helped her to stand. The man's body thumped on each step as he was dragged down the stairs.

"Are you alright?" Ruth asked.

The young woman's cheeks were bright red and her eyes were filled with tears. "This is not what I signed up for!" she cried.

Ruth watched the woman run across the landing and disappear down the stairs, the sound of her footsteps popping like firecrackers.

Running back into the bathroom, she pulled Junior onto the landing and coaxed him to the stairs. His wobbly legs awkwardly bent on the top step.

"Come on," she whispered. "You can do it."

At the bottom of the stairs was the wolfman, sitting on the last step.

Junior stopped.

"Shoo!" she said, waving her hand toward the man.

He stood up and moved into the hall.

She tugged at Junior's arm. "It's okay," she said.

She carefully pulled at him until they reached the bottom.

"Now stay still," she whispered. She reached into the bag and grabbed a shirt. "It's cold out there, let's put this on." She pushed his arm through the shirt sleeve, maneuvering the garment over his body. Buttoning the front, it hung like a bag on his thin frame. She steadied him and lifted his foot, slipping one pant leg over his pajamas. A clump of applesauce fell to the floor.

Junior bent down, reaching for the food.

"No, Junior," she said. "You'll get food soon."

She pulled a knit cap over his head and led him through the main room where the attendant was leaning against the front door.

"Where do ya think you're goin' with him?" he asked.

"Home," she said.

"Can't do that," he replied.

"Yes, I can," she said. She patted her coat pocket.

"With his getaway sticks, ya won't get far."

She took off her coat and slid it on Junior.

"They look for numbers on the lam, ya know," the attendant said. Then he opened the door.

She pulled Junior out of his cottage and onto the asylum grounds.

65

BROKEN TWIGS

Ruth rushed Junior down the asylum sidewalk. The coat hung loosely around his body, and she could see that he was shivering. "You'll be home soon," she said. His gangly legs stumbled like a three-legged animal struggling to keep up, but she kept pulling him forward. She searched the freezing grounds for activity and movement, but the area was quiet.

"We've got to hurry," she said, drawing her sweater closer to her body.

He began to slow.

"Junior, come on," she said. His knit cap drooped over one of his eyes, thrusting wool fibers into his sparse eyelashes. She pushed the cap up. His fist rubbed at his face and thumped his cheekbone.

"Let's go," she murmured.

His legs clumsily stepped forward.

"Halt!"

She looked at the empty baseball diamond. Two guards were charging across the field and pointing at her and Junior.

She yanked Junior into motion so forcefully he almost fell.

"Hurry!" she said. Hauling him between two cottages, she quickly pulled him over desiccated earth. He yelped and limped as they stepped on broken twigs and icy dead leaves.

"Faster, Junior," she said.

"Halt!" The voice was closer.

She tugged at his arm but he was slowing down. She yanked and pulled, but his wobbly legs were giving out. A large hand wrapped around her arm, abruptly stopping her movement and Junior's. She looked at the guard's hand gripping her arm. The cold of his glove seeped through her sweater as if she were sleeveless.

"Ma'am," he said. "Where are you going with this patient?" His peaked cap made his eyes appear sharp and fierce.

"I'm his mother," she said, yanking her arm from his grip. "I'm taking him home."

"Do you have his release papers?" he asked.

She looked at both guards. They were staring at her.

"No," she said, "but he's coming home with me."

"Sorry, ma'am. Not without papers."

66

SMALL PRINT

J unior sat on the metal examining table, the same one he sat upon his arrival.

"Finally," Ruth whispered. "We're meeting a doctor and I'll be able to take you home." She picked threadlike weeds from his socks and began to rub his cold feet. She thought about the clerk's expression when the guards escorted her into the registration office. How must she have looked walking into the room, disheveled and frantic and with a patient? But she was finally getting what she wanted.

She heard movements in the hall, but the door remained closed. Her hands rubbed Junior's feet faster and although he was still wearing her coat, he was shivering.

"Just a little bit longer," she said. "Then I'll get you in a hot bath."

The door opened and the same doctor that checked Junior in one month ago walked in. The lines of his forehead seemed deeper than she remembered.

"Doctor Frazer," she said. "I'm so glad to see you."

"What's going on?" he asked.

A nurse appeared in the doorway.

"I want to take my son home," she said.

"Why?" he asked.

"He's not getting the care he needs," she replied. "I can take better care of him myself." She watched the doctor as he crossed his arms, flattening a stethoscope against his stomach. And the nurse, she was suspiciously eyeing Junior.

"What do you mean?" he asked.

"He's not being cared for here," she said.

The doctor's chest rose. "Why do you say that?"

"Just look at him," she said. She removed Junior's cap. His thin hair was matted and hanging from his head like twisted twine. His sunken eye and pointy cheekbones made him look like an old man.

"Ma'am," he said, "you can't just take a patient out of here."

"But I just told you, he's not getting the care he needs." She touched Junior's face. His eyelids shut tightly. "And he hasn't had a bath in a long time," she said.

"We'll have to look into this," he replied. "We'll get back to you."

"I'm not leaving without him," she said. "His name is Walter Janikowski Junior. You checked him in a month ago, and I think you can check him out."

The doctor nodded to the nurse and said, "Please get the record." Then he turned to her. "Mrs. Janikowski, correct?"

"Yes."

"Now, what is this all about?"

"There's no help at his cottage. The patients, they're all sedated and neglected. And I just want to bring him home."

The doctor cleared his throat. "We have staff that work in every cottage," he said.

She studied his face. His forehead pinched in a way she did not like, deepening his wrinkles into his parched skin.

"Yesterday was the first day I could visit," she said. "And

there was only one nurse. Today, it was a different nurse and she left the building. Then another one was there but she left the building too."

He looked like he was listening, so she continued.

"And the rooms, they're filthy. There are too many patients crammed in. And rats! They're everywhere," she said. "It's hard to find an attendant. And when I do, they don't know what's going on."

The doctor raised his hand, like a judge. "That's enough," he said.

Junior grunted, twisting on the table. She turned toward her son. He was looking at the ceiling light. She patted his shoulder and rubbed his back.

The door opened and the nurse was back. She handed the doctor a file as she dutifully stood next to him, her hands clasped in front of her body.

"Mrs. Janikowski," he said, "from what I can see here, your son is getting the care he needs."

"What?"

"According to his record, he's doing just fine," he said.

"But the rooms. The smell. The lack of nurses." She stared at the doctor. "No. He is not doing *just fine.*"

The doctor stared back. The nurse's clasped hands dropped from her body, only to slowly cross over her chest.

"Have you been to Cottage Six?" Ruth asked.

The nurse's inhale was loud.

"*You* said he would get the care he needed. *You* said people here knew what they were doing. You said he would be just fine. This is *my* son," she said. "And there are a lot of other people's sons in here, and daughters, too. And they're not being cared for. No, he's coming home with me. Today." She stared at the doctor.

He looked at her, then, the nurse. "Nurse," he said, "leave us, please."

The nurse looked at Ruth, then walked out of the room and closed the door.

Ruth tightened the coat around Junior and put the cap back on his head.

"Mrs. Janikowski," he said.

She wasn't looking at the doctor, but knew he was moving closer to her.

"Mrs. Janikowski," he repeated. "You can't just take him home."

"Oh yes I can," she said. She pulled Junior from the table.

"No, you can't," he replied.

She stopped and faced the doctor. "Didn't you hear what I said? He hasn't been bathed, the living conditions are horrible, and I don't even know if he's been fed."

The doctor grabbed her arm. His grip was powerful.

She looked at his hand then his face. "Let go of me," she said.

"You can't take him out of here," he said.

"Why?"

"Because," he said. "This is a state institution and it's illegal."

"What do you mean *illegal?*"

"If you take this patient, they will find you *and* him and bring *him* back here. And you will be put in jail. What do you think will happen to him then?"

She stared at the doctor. His gaze pierced her eyes.

"When you signed the admittance papers," he continued, "you signed over your son."

Memories of small print and impatient signatures rushed to her mind.

The doctor opened the file. He tapped on one page.

"Is this your husband's signature?" He waved a paper with squiggle pen marks in her face.

"Yes, but—"

The door flung open. The nurse stood in the doorway and pointed at Junior.

"Right there," she said as two attendants came into the room.

Ruth hurled herself in front of Junior. The attendants grabbed at him as he squealed and punched.

"*No! Don't take him!*" she yelled, clawing at their powerful hands.

The doctor gripped her arms from behind, pulling her away from Junior. She watched the nurse strip the wool coat from Junior's body. "*Stop!*" Ruth cried.

The attendants strapped him to a gurney, his arms and legs swinging and kicking.

Ruth broke free from the doctor's grip and pounded on the back of one of the attendants.

"*Let him go!*" she yelled, her voice echoing in the hall.

The doctor pulled her away from the rolling cot.

"Ma'am! Please calm down!" The doctor's voice was forceful in her ear.

She screamed as she watched Junior being wheeled from her grasp—his screams and hers, crying in the same pitch.

"Please calm down," the doctor repeated. His grip tightened around her arms as he pulled her back into the room.

She twisted and turned but couldn't break free. Bending her leg, she kicked it backward, connecting with his shin. His grip pinched harder.

The nurse came back into the room. She was holding a silver tray in one hand and Ruth's coat in the other.

The doctor's breath felt hot on her neck as she spotted a syringe on the tray.

"I don't want to have to give this to you," he whispered.

She relaxed her arms. Then his grip loosened.

The nurse handed her the coat and left the room.

"Three signatures," he said.

"What?"

"You need three doctors to sign his release," he said.

She stared at the man. "Three doctors' signatures?"

He nodded.

"You can be the first," she said.

"First, a thorough examination is required to see if your son is fit for society."

"And then what?"

"I'm sorry," he said, "but I don't think he will ever qualify."

"We can't just *give* you the form," the clerk said. "A doctor must fill it out."

"Oh yes, of course," Ruth said.

The office behind the screened window looked chaotic, the same way it did the first time she saw it. The same stack of files, the same overflowing trash bins, and the same messy cabinets. The only difference was the clerk and registration nurse. She hadn't seen the same people more than twice.

"Is there anything else?" the clerk asked.

"Yes, can you open the hall door for me?"

"Ma'am, that's for admitting patients only," she said, then added, "I'm sorry, but I can't help you any further."

Ruth was heading toward the exit but stopped. Instead she took a seat in the waiting room and kept her eyes on the receiving door. Within moments, it opened and the next name was called. A girl seated across the room burst into tears.

"Poor dear." An old woman sitting next to Ruth paused her knitting needles. "Such a young girl," she said.

Ruth moved toward the edge of her seat and

unbuttoned her coat. She noticed the nurse at the door. She had not seen her before.

"Let me help you with that," the old woman said.

Ruth felt a tug at her coat sleeve. She removed her coat and folded it over her lap. The keys nearly fell out of her pocket but she caught them and quickly tucked them away.

The old woman stabbed her needles into a ball of yarn and asked, "Can you keep an eye on this for me?"

Ruth nodded and watched as she crossed the room and stepped to the front of the line. She was leaning into the screen and talking. Then she walked to the receiving door and it opened.

Moments later, she reappeared and took her seat.

"Thank you, dearie," she said. "I just couldn't hold it any longer."

Another name was called. Commotion filled the waiting room as another family walked to the receiving door.

Ruth stood up and put on her coat.

"Are you part of their family?" the old woman asked.

"Yes," she answered and merged into the group.

The nurse pointed to the examining room. "You can go in with your family," she said.

Ruth remained in the hallway, looking into the room. A young girl was sitting on the same table Junior had sat on.

"Can I use the powder room first?" she asked.

"End of hall, to the right."

The darkened hallway had an endless number of closed doors dotting the beige walls. Narrow transom windows topped each door, some dark, some lit. The sound of the nurse's shoes echoed in the hall as she disappeared into the registration office. Ruth's footsteps were quieter as she tiptoed in the opposite direction. Passing each door, she didn't hear any movement until she reached a door with a lit transom. The muffled sound of a man's voice was coming from behind the door. Despite his hushed tone, a level of superiority was clear.

She leaned in.

"Yes, sir," he said. "I understand, sir. Thank you, sir."

Leaning in further, her hand touched the door. It swung open before she could stop it and an older man sitting behind a desk was placing the receiver back on his telephone.

"How did you get in here?" he questioned. His voice was startled, but the superiority was still there. She looked around the elegant room. Blue and gold wallpaper lined the space and deer heads, oil paintings, and diplomas hung on each wall. On his desk sat an elephant tusk inkwell and next to it his title plaque.

"Pardon me," she said. "I'm Mrs. Walter Janikowski. I'm hoping you can help me."

The man adjusted his kingly chair, swirling a crystal whiskey glass in her direction. She watched his eyes rove over her dirty coat.

"What is it?" he asked.

The plaque proclaimed he was the superintendent, and she was unsure of where to begin.

"What is it?" he repeated.

She stuttered but her explanation came out. She told him about Junior and her wish to bring him home. She didn't want to leave anything out, but couldn't help notice his ivory pen and the speedy way it tapped against a notebook.

"Ma'am," he said, cutting her off. "I'm sorry for your troubles, but I'm very busy."

"Yes, of course," she said, stepping closer to his desk. "I just need one little favor."

The handle to his pince-nez disappeared between his thumb and finger. He lifted the eye glasses from his nose and tossed them on his notebook. "Ma'am, do you have an appointment?" he asked. His bloodshot eyes looked dry, so dry as if they would crumble and fall out of his eye sockets.

"I just need a signature for my son's release," she said. "That's all."

The sound of his sigh was loud as he shook his head. His hand slowly moved toward a small black box on his desk.

"This will be the easiest thing you do all day," she added.

His index finger extended and pushed at a button on the receptacle.

"Wouldn't it be nice to have one less patient in here?" she asked.

He rose from his chair. He was tall and round.

"Ma'am. You'll have to make an appointment," he said.

"Of course," she replied. "I already have an appointment."

Putting the eyeglass piece on, he checked a small calendar on his desk.

"When is your appointment?" he asked.

"Well, it's not until January."

He looked at her then stepped past her to the door. She watched him peer out into the hall and motion with his hand.

"Please," she said. "I need to get my son out of here."

His hand signaled faster.

She cleared her throat. "Forgive me, but, like I said, I've been here every day for the past week, feeding and caring for my son. All I need is your signature."

The superintendent walked back to his desk. She watched his every move and noticed he was watching hers.

"He's strapped to a wheelchair," she said, repeating what she already told him, but in less pleasant terms. "Because no one is watching him, they don't bathe him or feed him, the rooms are filthy, it smells to high heaven, and there's rats. I can never find anyone to help." She felt stinging in her eyes as she stared at the man.

His chest rose, but he remained silent.

"And there are too many patients to a room, not enough blankets," she continued. "Their clothes need to be washed. Please. Help me."

Footsteps pounded in the hall, becoming louder.

"Please," she said.

He exhaled loudly and plopped into his chair. His powerful demeanor sank away as he slouched into the seat.

"I don't even know what patient you are talking about," he said.

"My son," she whispered. "His name is Walter Janikowski Junior, and I want to take him home with me. Today."

An attendant appeared in the doorway.

The superintendent leaned forward, his hands momentarily covering his face, pulling his skin down. Finally, he rose from his chair and motioned to the attendant to follow him into the hall.

"Just a moment," he said to her and closed the door.

She looked at his desk. A short silver lamp curled over his notebook. The ivory pen rested on top, pointing to scribbled writing. She moved the book. The page was empty except for two words.

Budget cuts.

Her finger slid over the writing, smudging a blob of ink from the capital B. The tiny black stain was like a prisoner's tattoo. She moved the book back, next to a black and white photograph of the superintendent with his family. The sound of movement in the hall pulled her attention away. She looked at the door. It clicked and opened.

The superintendent reappeared and said, "Mrs. Janikowski, we are trying to locate your son's record. I'll have to get back to you."

"But all I need is for you to sign a release form. I'll take care of the rest," she said, patting her pocket.

He plopped into his chair and grabbed his whiskey. "We have to examine the patient first before any recommendations can be made."

"When will that be?"

"Maybe next week."

"Can't you just sign the paper?" she asked. "My son is just fine."

"Ma'am, this is a state institution. We are monitored by the governor. I'm sorry, but we can't do that. My hands are tied."

In the bathroom of Cottage Six, Ruth kicked a bloody bandage into a corner. Junior wiggled as she slid his pajama bottoms off. His legs were skinny and his diaper was deep yellow and sagging. She unclipped the cloth and tossed it into the stained tub. His dirty flesh was inflamed with a patchwork of pus and scabs. She turned on the faucet, letting the brown water run, but it only cleared to a dirty orange. He flinched as she sponged his skin with a damp cloth.

"It's okay, Junior," she said. It took several washings before she removed the dirt, but in some areas, his skin looked stained. "Now, don't move."

Grabbing a towel from her bag, she unfurled it and spread it over the floor, then centered a clean diaper on it. Pushing on his shoulders, she maneuvered him downward until he toppled onto the towel.

"Let's get you over the diaper," she said. She pulled at the diaper, arranging it under his bottom. "Now, lay down."

He squirmed and thrashed as she tried to stretch his limbs over the cloth, one at a time, but he fought her every move. The towel bunched up, mixing with hairballs and rat poop and forcing her to pull the edges straight again. Resting her knee over one of his legs, she pulled the other one down.

He wiggled and twisted and rolled off the towel.

She positioned him back into place, holding him down with her legs and grabbing a corner of the diaper. Quickly, she swaddled his body and clipped the cloth into place but his newly washed back was dirty again.

G usting November wind rattled the waiting room windows. Even though the day was just starting, the outside temperature was not rising. Ruth's coat collar was drawn close to her neck, but she was not cold. The waiting room was overcrowded and warm and an enormous man sitting next to her concealed her from the registration window. She peeked around his unusually large head. The waiting room line was long, and two people were standing at the window. Squinting through the veil of her hat, she tried to identify the clerk, but the screen was too grainy. The receiving door opened and a blonde nurse stood in the doorway. A clipboard hid her nose and mouth, but Ruth did not recognize the young woman's eyes.

"Kaczka. Um, Mrs. Ludwik Kaczka." The nurse's words were quiet and sounded like a question, but when she repeated the name, her voice was louder.

Ruth felt the room stir.

"Nie! Nie!" A woman was yelling in Polish, resisting a man's attempt to lift her from her chair.

Ruth watched as the man wrangled her free from her seat. People sitting nearby jumped from their chairs, avoiding her swinging arms. In a moment, the crowd fell silent as the man dragged her toward the receiving door.

Ruth looked at the nurse. The clipboard was lowered, exposing a frightened face as she stood motionless waiting for the man to pull the woman into the hallway. Even though the door closed, the woman's screaming could still be heard.

The occupants of the room reorganized and the enormous man rolled back and forth and shifted in his chair. His fleshy leg overflowed onto Ruth's seat, touching her thigh with his cold, heavy limb and forcing her to the edge of her seat. The receiving door opened again.

A loose strand of blonde hair was hanging over the nurse's nose and before she could say the next name, Ruth was out of her seat and walking toward the door.

"Excuse me," Ruth said. "Could I use the powder room?"

The nurse's eyes didn't seem to blink.

"The ladies' room. The bathroom. Could I use it?" Ruth asked.

The nurse seemed unsure.

Ruth pushed past her and stepped into the hall.

"Ma'am?"

The quietness of the nurse's voice alarmed Ruth. It was only her and the nurse in the hallway, and the door to the waiting room was closing.

"Yes?" Ruth replied.

"I'm sorry," the nurse said. "But I don't know where the powder room is."

"Oh." Ruth stared at the young woman. "I'll find it," she said. She started to walk down the hallway but stopped and turned around. "Is it possible to get a release form?"

The nurse's eyes widened.

"A blank one?" Ruth continued. "The doctor's gonna

sign my son's release form today, and I'm sure he'll be happy if I have the form ready."

The nurse nodded.

"I'll wait right here," Ruth said. She watched the nurse disappear through a side door, leaving the endless hallway deserted. She leaned against the cold wall, studying which transom windows were lit.

Within moments, the office door reopened, and the young nurse was approaching her. "Here," she said. She was holding a folded piece of paper and offering it to Ruth. "I was able to find this without help."

Ruth grabbed the paper. "Thank you," she said.

"Well?" the nurse asked.

Ruth looked at her.

"Aren't you going to use the powder room?"

"Oh. Right. Yes. Thank you."

71

HUM OF APPROVAL

Opulent sconces and a fancy gilded sofa in the women's lounge contradicted the erratic waiting room at the end of the hallway. Ruth looked around the small space and listened for movement from the bathroom stall. It was quiet. Sheer pink lampshades anchored on each side of a gold leaf mirror complemented a rosy, golden tapestry of plump women bathing in a stream. She lifted the veil of her velvet hat. The room brightened but the light revealed scrapes and gouges on a once graceful marble counter. Reaching into her pocket, she pulled out the folded piece of paper and carefully opened it. Her hand slid over the creases, flattening the document. The scent of the musky paper mingled with a potpourri of rose soap, creating a sense of relaxation in the tranquil room.

She was studying the blank spaces of the release form and the three expectant signature lines when the hinges of the lounge door creaked. She glanced in the mirror. The reflection of a haggard woman appeared, bringing with it a wave of body odor. Specks of dirt covered her face and greasy hair hung in her eyes.

Ruth quickly folded the paper, placing it in her coat pocket, next to the ring of keys.

The woman disappeared into the toilet stall. She heard a loud stream of pee splashing into the bowl followed by coughing and hacking. The room filled with a whoosh of the flush and the stall door opened.

Ruth fussed with a brown curl around her hat, only to slowly rearrange it as she watched the reflection of the room. Shuffling from the stall, the disheveled woman passed the sink, stumbling into the hallway without closing the door.

"This way please," came a voice from the hall.

Ruth watched the woman dutifully follow the directions, disappearing behind a door marked *Lecture Room* and leaving the hallway empty. Then she looked at the transom windows and was about to step into the hall when a guard entered from the other end, heading her way. She stayed in the lounge, spying on the man until she was alone again. She crept back into the hall and could hear voices coming from the Lecture Room. The partly opened door displayed the haggard woman strapped to a gurney. A wad of gauze had been stuffed in her mouth and she was shaking uncontrollably. Huge dome lights hovered over her body and a group of doctors huddled around the gurney and the superintendent stood with the group. A bald man with a goatee was speaking. She strained to make out the words but couldn't. Next to the man was a nurse, holding a silver tray. Plucking a long thin instrument from the plate, the bald man held it in the air to show his colleagues. A collective hum of approval wafted into the hall. The man then grabbed a small hammer and held it aloft. He circled the patient, stopping at her head and nodding to the nurse. The nurse's hands wrapped around the woman's head, tilting her chin to the lights.

An announcement was made to the group. They

crowded closer to the gurney. Ruth's view was blocked. Within seconds, the group gasped. One of the men grabbed his stomach and lurched backward, giving her a view. The gap in the circle revealed the bald man had pushed the long instrument inside the woman's eye socket. He began to tap with the hammer, pounding it deeper into her head. Ruth gagged. She fell back into the hallway and rushed to the lounge.

72

BURNING

Partially digested eggs and coffee hurled from Ruth's mouth, splashing into the toilet. Another roiling heave lurched her stomach, causing her to spew forward, releasing a second wave. She gripped the toilet, fighting for control, but it was too late. A third wave arrived burning her throat with acid and pouring bile into the water. The lounge door creaked open, accompanied by a trace of floral perfume. Her gag reflex threatened again. Her eyes closed as she willed herself into a sense of calm. Wiping her mouth, she slowly stood up. The tiny space momentarily swayed, then stopped. She walked out of the stall.

Standing in front of the mirror was the nurse from the Lecture Room, and her head twisted from side to side, admiring a reflection of well-groomed eyebrows and stylish curls. Her manicured hands twisted a lipstick tube, circling red color around her puckered lips. Ruth stepped to the mirror and looked at the nurse. Their gazes connected.

"Pardon me," Ruth said, nudging her way to the sink.

The nurse puckered her lips again and adjusted her white cap then walked out of the door.

Ruth watched the nurse enter the superintendent's office. The transom above the door was dark.

73

BLACK AND WHITE

"All I'm asking for is for you to sign this release form," Ruth said.

The superintendent shifted uncomfortably, but she kept her eye on him as she circled both him and the nurse in his office.

"It's just your signature," she continued.

His office looked completely different in dim lighting, intimate and cozy, but the black and white family portrait was still on his desk.

"Besides," she said. "It will be one less patient for you to worry about," She adjusted the family photograph, letting his desk lamp light bounce off the glass frame. His glare shifted from her face, to the photograph, then the nurse.

"Could you excuse us, please," he said, nodding to the woman.

She scoffed and huffed and left the room. Then he shut the door.

Ruth watched him lumber to his desk. The framed photograph reflected his slow movements.

"It won't do you any good," he sighed.

"What do you mean?" she asked.

"Having me sign the form," he said. "It won't do you any good." His heavy body plopped into his chair.

"But all I need is three signatures," she said. "It says so right here." The blank page shook with each tap of her finger.

"Yes, but even with three signatures, you won't get your son out."

"I don't understand." Her grip tightened on the release form.

"The Director," he said. "He will have the final say. And, well . . . frankly, he won't sign it."

"But why?" she asked.

She saw him glance at the door then back at her.

"It just doesn't happen," he said. "People do not get released from here." His eyes closed as he leaned back in his chair. His breath became loud and steady, making her wonder if he was falling asleep.

"What do you mean people don't get released? This isn't a prison."

His eyelids jolted open, then his stare locked on her face. A long steady breath sailed from his lungs as his fingers reached for the elephant tusk inkwell.

"Here," he said. He waved his hand, motioning for the document.

Rushing to his side, she placed the empty form on his desk and pointed to one of the blank signature lines.

He scribbled a swirl, dotting the black gibberish with a thump. "If you really want your son outta here," he said, "you'd have a better chance getting him transferred to another asylum than getting him released."

She grabbed the signed form.

"Good luck," he said.

74

ALWAYS HUNGRY

Ruth plunked a spoonful of oatmeal into Junior's open mouth. The can of marbles quietly rested in his lap but his legs started to bounce, rolling the wheelchair away from the second floor landing window. She set the oatmeal can on the floor. It was almost gone, and no matter how much she brought, Junior was always hungry. The old nurse with the skunk hair was working. She was the only nurse Ruth had seen more than once in the entire month she had been visiting the asylum. Most days, she couldn't find a nurse, only attendants. But today, the old woman was there, standing at the file cabinet. Ruth looked at her. She seemed to be reading something, except she never turned a page.

"How long have you been working here?" Ruth asked.

The nurse's eyes narrowed, hiding every bit of the white. "Why do you need to know that?" she asked.

"I haven't seen a doctor in this building since I've been coming here," she said. "When do they show up?"

"Ma'am, I don't know." The nurse's words always sounded sharp and abrupt, even when Ruth tried to ask her about her family and hobbies.

"Have you ever seen a doctor in this cottage?" she asked.

"Stop asking questions," the nurse said. Despite her skinny frame and fragile body, she stomped around the landing like she weighed three hundred pounds.

"But," Ruth said, "these patients, they look so unhealthy. And skinny."

A loud sound from the first floor caused Junior to jump. The can of marbles fell off his lap and knocked the oatmeal can over.

"Oh no!" Ruth cried. "That's all I've got!" She landed on her knees scrambling and scooping the spilled oats and slinging them back into the can along with dirt from the floor and woodchips. Her vision blurred with tears as she looked at the dirty mixture of oats. The nurse's white shoes appeared in her eyesight, but she couldn't lift her head to look at the woman.

"The doctors rarely come here," the nurse murmured. Her voice was as quiet as a grave digger. "But they have physician housing."

Ruth blinked away her tears and looked up at the nurse.

The old woman's eyes were darting around the landing as she leaned closer to Ruth. "At the back of the asylum grounds."

75

THE GATES

Icy squalls swirled around Ruth as she stood on the front porch of the doctor's brick house. Sheer curtains covered the door window, but she could still see the doctor's wife on the inside and the woman did not look happy.

Ruth smiled and nodded.

The door opened slightly. "Can I help you?" the woman asked.

"Is your husband home?" Ruth replied. A sliver of heat seeped out of the door and she couldn't resist huddling closer.

"What do you want?" the woman asked. The door seemed to be inching closed.

"I'm hoping your husband will sign my son's release form," she said.

The woman pulled her dress collar closer to her neck. "This is a private home," she said. "And the gates are supposed to be locked." Ruth watched the woman's eyes rove over the yard. "How did you get back here?" she asked.

Ruth rubbed the side of her coat, pushing the thorny

keys to the bottom of her pocket. "One of the guards," she said.

"Which one?" The woman's eyes were scanning the yard again.

"It doesn't matter. Is your husband home?" she asked.

The woman pulled at the door, but Ruth's overboot was in the way. She watched as the woman glanced down, then up, but she did not move her boot. "Is he home or not?" she asked.

Suddenly she felt a sharp pain stab at her shin, causing her leg to retract and the door to slam shut.

A folded plaid blanket was draped over the backseat of the taxi, but the wool fabric was ice cold. The outside temperature remained around freezing that week, and Ruth was huddled on the backseat. Her arms wrapped across her chest and she rubbed her crossed legs together, but her teeth were chattering.

"Where to, ma'am?" Big brown eyes filled the rearview mirror.

"415 Superior Street," she replied.

The cabbie's bushy eyebrows floated upward. "Downtown?" he asked.

She nodded. She knew Walter was unhappy she was out, and she thought of the ways he tried to convince her to stay home. How he talked of the icy roads and closed businesses, but his wishes would not stop her.

The taxi lurched into gear, pushing her body against the seat.

"Sure is a cold one, eh?" the cabbie said. "And they say snow's a comin' and a lot."

Her neighborhood gave way to territory last seen when she and Margaret were teenage girls. Back then, the downtown storefronts looked different. They showcased dresses and shoes in every window. Ruth recalled her mother saying the girls would someday marry and their husbands would buy them luxurious fabrics and fashionable shoes. It had been a warm summer day. Ruth wore her favorite white dress with a yellow ribbon as a belt. It made her waist appear smaller than Margaret's. She remembered the matching lace gloves and how her reflection looked like a picture from a magazine and how her life was going to be perfect.

"Ma'am? Ma'am?" The taxi driver's hand pressed on the back of the seat, twisting his head toward her. His gentle eyes contrasted sharply with his flattened nose. He looked like a boxer who had been in one too many fights. "We're here," he said.

A prestigious three-story ashlar building loomed against the sidewalk. Large, arched windows supported decorative stone urns that dotted the roofline, and on the front of the building etched words announced the local newspaper.

"Your article, Mr. Pinkston."

He liked the way the woman said his name. She seemed worried about something, almost nervous. The newsroom was warm, but she didn't take off her coat and her gloved hands kept fidgeting with her hat as she sat by his desk. His coffee had a shot of whiskey in it and he asked her if she wanted some, but her brown waves bounced as she shook her head no. "Which article?" he asked.

She finally removed her gloves and her hat came to a rest on her lap. "The one about the asylums," she replied. "Do you know where a good one is?" Her voice was soft but strong.

"A good asylum?" he asked. *Was she joking?* "No, I don't," he said. "Why?" He leaned back in his chair and fixed his eyes on her. She was beautiful. But she looked lost. And there was a deep sorrow in her eyes.

"My son." She cleared her throat. "My son is at the asylum in town."

A long low whistle blew from his lips, but he hoped she didn't hear it.

"I've been trying to get him out," she continued. "But they say transferring him would be easier."

Her eyes bounced around the newsroom, not in a shifty criminal way, but in a scared rabbit sort of way.

"So, you want to find a better asylum?" he asked.

She nodded.

He doubted she understood the magnitude of the institutional problems or what she was asking for. Her eyelashes blinked what appeared to be the beginning of tears, and he leaned forward in his chair, watching her dab her eyes with a handkerchief. Her hands looked rough and chapped.

He opened a drawer and pulled out a bottle and two shot glasses.

"Here," he said, handing her a small amount of the brown liquid. He watched as she brought the glass to her nose and took a tiny sip. Her face grimaced at the fire that must've been burning her throat.

"Thank you," she coughed.

"Let me see what I've got," he said. He searched the mess of files on his desk. He wanted to find her a miracle but pulled out a piece of paper with scribbles and Xs on it.

"Mrs. Janikowski," he said. He leaned toward her again. Her scent matched the beauty of her face. He wanted to tell her a lie. To make her feel better. Instead he said, "I must be honest with you. All the asylums are bad. The population for each sanitarium far exceeds the capacity. There is not enough staff to care for the overcrowding. And, well, the conditions—" he abruptly stopped.

"I know. I've been there," she said. Her tears were coming back.

"You might try the asylum at the state capital," he said. "You know, maybe having the governor so close, they might take better care of patients there. But I just don't know."

After their conversation, he drove her to the asylum, the

local one they talked about. The one that was just like others. The one her son was in.

"Thank you for driving me," she said. Her voice was quiet and sad.

"Well, it's too cold for you to stand at the bus stop," said. "And you probably would've arrived after visiting hours."

Her beautiful brown waves swayed under her hat as she nodded her thanks.

"You're a good man, Mr. Pinkston" she said.

TOWARD THE LIGHT

"I need to have my son transferred to the asylum in Columbus," Ruth said.

The clerk searched a drawer in a file cabinet, returning with a piece of paper. "Here you go," she said, pushing the document through the opened window screen.

Ruth stared at the empty form. Her rehearsed speech annulled and the keys in her pocket not needed. She grabbed the piece of paper.

"Fill out the top," the clerk said. "We'll do the rest."

"How many doctors need to sign this?" she asked.

"One."

"Just one?"

"Yes, just one," the clerk replied.

The single sheet of paper was covered with several sentences and blank lines.

"Do you have a pen I can use?"

"There's one in the waiting room."

In the late afternoon, the once-crowded space was nearly empty. She looked for a pen, but only saw empty chairs, a handful of people, and the Victrola. She took a seat and rummaged through her bag, removing two pairs of socks, a diaper, baby food, and a metal meat pounder. She leaned over and scanned the floor.

"Here," a man's voice said.

She looked up at an old man, his puffy white hair looked like a halo of cotton and in his hand was a pen.

"Thank you," she said.

His twinkling eyes twitched behind spider-cracked spectacles as he handed her the pen.

The loud speakers crackled in the room and fragmented words announced the registration office was closed for the day and would reopen tomorrow at 10 a.m., weather permitting. Half of the room turned dark.

She moved toward the window, propping the form against the frosty windowsill. The pen slid over bumps and cracks as she filled in her son's name. Holding the paper up to the window, she inspected the blank space labeled *Physician's Signature*. That one would soon be filled in, too. The remaining lights turned off and the winter skies added little light to the darkened space.

She knew the old man was still in the room, watching her.

"Ma'am," he said. "Time to get outta here. We're about to get more snow."

She handed him the pen and he seemed to be waiting for her, but she paused and said, "I need to use the powder room." She walked to the hall door and to her surprise, it was unlocked.

Bundled workers were rushing toward her and out the door but she was going in the opposite direction. All the doors were closed and all the transom windows were dark except for the superintendent's office. Gripping the half-filled-in form, she walked toward the light. Her rehearsed speech of convincing and, if needed—threatening—words floated in her mind.

With the signed form, she would convince the guards

that her husband was going to transfer Junior and there was no need for him to remain in the asylum any longer. He had been there for almost two months and now, she was going to bring him home. She approached the superintendent's door. He would have no choice but to sign the form because Junior was coming home with her. She was going to make sure of it.

A nother hour and he was off duty. A long weekend. Just him and his whiskey. Unless the snow got too bad and he was called back to work. Living on the asylum grounds had its perks. Free housing. Easy commute. But as a guard, they always expected him to work overtime, as if he didn't have anything better to do. He set his coffee cup in the sink, still full. Leaving the breakroom, he stepped into the hall, and the late winter afternoon left it dark and cold. Nurses and attendants, rushing to beat the expectant snow, bumped into him. One rang his funny bone.

"Have a good weekend." The unexpected acknowledgment came from one of the butter-and-egg men.

He nodded back and watched the genius group scurry down the hall, like rats running from a flooding basement. The hallway emptied, except for someone staring into the superintendent's office. A woman. Didn't she know the super had been given the pink slip? It was said he took a powder because of budget cuts, but he knew better. She was probably another one of the bum's flames. He was sure she didn't know how the boozehound flipped his wig when they escorted him out, and how he said the asylum would go belly up without him. He'd have to break it to her gently.

"Excuse me, ma'am," he said, "You can't be back here un—" It was her. The lady from Cottage Six. Her eyes were still beautiful and still sad. And now filled with tears. "Ma'am. Did you find your son?" he asked.

"Where's?" Her gloved finger pointed at the empty office and her hand was shaking.

"He was pink slipped," he said.

She looked at him. He didn't want to look at her eyes anymore.

"Why?" she said, her voice was barely a whisper.

"Budget cuts," he answered.

T wo white dice came to a rest on the board game. George watched Anna stomp her wooden pawn seven spaces and land directly on his lot.

"That'll be two thousand dollars," he said. He flung his open palm in front of her face and wiggled it.

"But George," she said. "I don't have it."

"That's what the rent is with my hotel," he replied, wiggling his palm again and eyeing her small stack of colorful fake money.

"But I don't have it!" she repeated.

"Then you lose. I win," he said.

"Ma! George cheated again!"

"I don't have t' cheat to beat a number like you," he said. He glanced at his mother, waiting for *the look*, but she was busy, hunched over the living room desk, writing something, over and over. Just as he thought she would never stop, her pencil broke. She picked up the fractured tip, looking at it as if she didn't know what it was, then tossed it into a waste basket full of crumpled stationary. She seemed to be comparing two pieces of paper, holding them up, side by side, like a nun looking for cheaters. Her sigh was louder than Anna's. She stood up and grabbed her coat from the rack.

"Ma. You want me to sharpen that for you?" He wanted to do something for her. Anything to take the sorrow from her eyes. "Ma?"

She looked at him as if she just realized they were in the same room.

He jumped up, accidentally kicking the game, knocking the wooden houses across the board.

"See? You're cheating," Anna said.

He looked at the piece of paper on the desk. It was filled with scribbles, the same thing written over and over. He picked up the pencil and said, "I'll sharpen this."

The kitchen was cold as he walked to the backdoor, no oven turned on, no cookies on the counter, and no supper cooking. His boots were sitting in a puddle of water from earlier, the insides still warm. Slipping the pencil behind his ear, he fastened his coat and stepped outside. Glacial temperatures iced his cheeks and the tidy stepping stones of summer were now buried under a foot of snow. The frosty surface crunched under his boots, his foot plunging through fluff to the frozen ground below. His father's workshop was steps away. Gusty winds lifted his coat collar, slapping his face as if he just got caught skipping class. His bare hand landed on the frozen doorknob, stinging his skin. The darkened room was frigid. Fumbling for the light string, his fingers hooked onto the stiff cord. The workshop transformed with the light.

Heaps of junk cluttered the room. Junk he wanted to look at and junk he wanted to fix. Cans of broken pencils and gadget-filled cigar boxes fascinated him, almost making him forget what he went in there for. Pulling open a cabinet drawer, his eyes landed on an assortment of screwdrivers, arranged methodically according to size and head. Each instrument lay equidistant from one another, forming a perfect right angle cut off at the tip. At the back of the drawer was an old photograph turned upside down. He picked it up. The corners were worn and there was a tear at the bottom, but there they were. His mother and Junior. She was cuddling him when he was a baby.

Tears welled in his eyes. He couldn't remember if he had ever seen her look this happy or hopeful. He returned the photograph to the drawer. His icy breath puffed the air as he looked at the disheveled room. Between a greasy oil can and an old iron was a shiny cylinder. He jabbed the broken pencil into the black hole, cranking and grinding the lead stick to a sharpened point for this mother.

COERCING A SENSE OF CALM

"**M**a'am," the clerk said. "There's a mistake." Ruth froze. She thought the doctor's signature looked perfect on the transfer document. She thought she would be taking Junior home with her today. She thought this nightmare was over. "What do you mean, there's a mistake?" she asked.

"Your telephone number," the clerk said. "It's missing."

She stared at the woman. The form was bouncing underneath her tapping finger, as she pointed to the blank space. "See?" the clerk said, "Right here."

Ruth reached inside the registration window, grabbing the form and a pen from the clerk's counter. She scribbled the letters and numbers of her telephone, but they were so shaky, she had to scribble it out and start again. She felt the clerk staring at her. "They say we've got more snow coming our way," Ruth said, coercing a sense of calm. She slid the paper back to the nurse. "Will my husband and I be able to take him right now?" she asked.

"No," the clerk replied. "We have a truck that transports patients."

"Well, there's no need for that," Ruth said. "We can take him now."

"No, that's not allowed. He will be transported by someone here."

"When?"

"First the paperwork must be processed. Then we'll telephone you to let you know."

"How long does that take?"

The nurse looked at Ruth and the line behind her.

"Ma'am," she began, "we have a lot to do here. I said, we'll call you when it's processed."

R uth knew Liberty Theater was across the street, but she couldn't see it. A white curtain of snow shrouded the window and no matter how often the snowplows ran, the city was brought to a halt, including the bus service. She stood at the living room window. Snow drifted over the front porch, swirling up to the railing in defiance of George's shoveling. The cast-iron radiator, clanging heat into the drafty space, was covered with hats and gloves.

Her steps echoed in the quiet room as she crossed the floor and picked up the telephone. The dial tone, the same one from earlier, hummed its dull, flat sound in her ear. She was sick of hearing it. Her finger flicked the telephone switch, pushing it up and down.

"Operator, may I help you?" The twangy response jolted her back into the room.

"Are the lines still working?" she asked.

"Yes, they are," the woman replied. "Did you need help placing a call?"

"No, not yet, thank you," she said and hung up the telephone. She walked back to the window but didn't know what she was hoping to see. *Junior walking home?* She touched the icy glass. Her fingers traced the frilly frost, as if drawing a path would lead him back to her. The blizzard put a stop to her visits. The telephone was her only hope, except it wasn't ringing. She had called the asylum every day that week, sometimes two or three times a day. She knew the clerks' voices by heart, and she didn't have to keep repeating her story. She kept telling them the only thing she needed to know was what date Junior was going to be transferred. But their answers were all the same. She would be notified when the paperwork was completed.

Pressing her finger into the number five, she turned the dial to the finger stop. It clicked then rotated back, ready for the next number. She continued to dial until the tone changed.

"Toledo Asylum for the Insane, how can I direct your call?"

"The registration office, please."

The black telephone cord twisted around her hand and looped around her fingers, making them colder than they already were.

"One moment, please."

A clerk got on the line, a voice she recognized. She knew their conversation was going to be the same, but she explained again anyway. She tried to get an answer. She tried to make the clerk tell her Junior's transfer date, but the woman said they still didn't know.

"How can I direct your call?"

"Registration office, please," Ruth said.

"Ma'am. I told you the last time you called," the operator said. "Registration is closed due to the holidays and won't open until next Tuesday."

"There's got to be someone there." she said. "What about a nurse? Or janitor?"

"Ma'am, there's hardly anyone here today."

"Please," Ruth said. "Find me someone. Anyone. Please."

The voice on the other end went silent. She wondered if the woman hung up on her.

"Okay," the operator said. "Let me see what I can do. Please hold."

Ruth touched her forehead. It seemed warm. The thought of Junior, cold and hungry, was making her sick.

"Ma'am?" A voice, one she didn't recognize, was on the other end of the line.

"Yes?"

"I'm Mrs. Miller, one of the nurses from the

administration building. What sort of emergency are you having?"

"My son. I need to know if he's been transferred to the asylum in Columbus. In the capital."

"Is this an emergency?" she asked.

"Yes."

"What is your son's name."

"Walter Janikowski Junior."

"Let me look for his record. Please hold."

Ruth closed her eyes and waited.

"Ma'am?" The woman returned to the telephone quicker than she thought she would.

"Yes," she replied.

"You said Janikowski. Walter Janikowski, correct?" the nurse asked.

"Yes. Correct."

"Well, according to this record, he was transferred Thursday night."

"What do you mean he was transferred Thursday night? I thought someone was going to telephone me?"

"I don't know about that, I'm just reading what the record says."

"Why didn't someone call me?"

"Ma'am, I don't know," the woman said. "We don't have a lot of help in here, and we're doing the best we can."

"I can't believe this!" Ruth said. "Do you have their telephone number? I want to call them!"

"We do not have a telephone number for family, but we have an address. You can write them."

PART V

1951

Time is a very precious gift of God; so precious that it is only given to us moment by moment.
— AMELIA EDITH HUDDLESTON BARR

OUT OF HER GRASP

T he wooden planks of the living room floor were worn, especially by the window.

"He'll come today," Walter said. "You know what they say, neither snow nor rain or, well, temperature."

Ruth knew he was trying to lighten the mood before leaving for work, but she couldn't smile. She wanted to be washing the clothes or doing the dishes, but her body wouldn't move. The weather had been horrendous. The beginning of the year had seemed colder than December and now, in the middle of January, they were buried in snow. The whole city had stopped. The last time she saw Junior was at the beginning of December. He was cold and skinny, and she was sure no one was taking care of him. She hadn't slept in weeks. And now he was out of her grasp, transferred over the holidays, when the asylum was closed to visitors.

"I don't understand," she said. "Why can't I telephone the Columbus Asylum. What are they afraid of?"

"Everything's fine," Walter said. "I'm sure that asylum is better. After all, the governor's down there."

The Columbus Asylum was a three-hour drive away. If only she could figure out a way to get down there.

"I might be home early," he said. "They've got us comin' in late to save on heat. The Big Cheese has short arms and long pockets."

She watched Walter leave and the Hudson roll out of the driveway onto the icy street. Her eyes peered down the sidewalk, waiting for a man in blue. The day advanced and the weather declined first to gray and dreary, then it started to snow. Not one car passed her house all day, and the sidewalk remained empty. The snow began to fall faster.

Suddenly, he appeared. The unmistakable uniform of a postman, even under a thick coat, hat, and earmuffs. His body angled into the snow, a full sack of mail on his back. Three freezing envelopes were placed in her hand. One return address caught her attention: State of Ohio. Columbus Asylum.

85

TO ADVISE YOU

State of Ohio
Columbus Asylum
Columbus 14, Ohio
December 28, 1950

Dear Mrs. Janikowski:

This is to advise you that your <u>son, Walter</u> has been admitted to the Columbus Asylum.

At present <u>he</u> is residing on the admissions ward where the necessary preliminary examinations are being made.

You may visit <u>him</u> on any week day from 8:30 A.M to 4:00 P.M. and the fourth Sunday of each month, after Jan. 28, 1950. Please feel free to talk with our Social Worker at the time of your visit.

We shall be glad to have you write to <u>Walter</u>

at any time. The address is: 401 West Broad
Street, Columbus, Ohio.

Sincerely,
Roger S. Gates, M.D.
Superintendent

By: (Mrs.) Sara F. Williams
Receiving Hospital

86

NOT ALLOWED

State of Ohio
Columbus Asylum
Columbus 14, Ohio
January 3, 1951

Dear Mrs. Janikowski:

In regard to your letter of December 28th,
we have admitted Walter to Department 2. Mr.
Jones is the supervisor of this department
and we have referred your letter to him.

After our patients are admitted, they
receive thorough physical and psychological
examinations, and we are not able to tell
you the future plans for Walter until these
are completed.

You may visit on any weekday except
holidays, and on the fourth Sunday of every

month. You are not allowed to visit until
Walter has been here thirty days.

Thank you for your interest in Walter and in
our Asylum.

Sincerely,
Roger S. Gates, M.D.
Superintendent

By: Violet Baker
Social Case Worker

ANYTHING THAT HE MAY NEED

State of Ohio
Columbus Asylum
Columbus 14, Ohio
January 22, 1951

Dear Mrs. Jarnikowski:

Your letter of January 16th has been
referred to the Social Service Department.
Mr. Jones says he will be glad to buy some
pop for Walter or anything that he may need.

Very truly yours,
Roger S. Gates, M.D.
Superintendent

By: Violet Baker
Social Case Worker

FADED CIRCLES

Ruth stared at her misspelled name at the top of the letter. Was it a simple mistake? Or were they careless? She immediately pulled out the desk chair and sat down.

The next morning, she waited for the mailman, her letter stamped and ready. The scratched wooden floor had two faded circles that marked her place by the window. She stood and waited.

He finally arrived, bundled and sniffling. "Mornin', Mrs. Janikowski, or is it afternoon?" he asked.

"Can't tell too much these days," she said, looking at the sky. More snow fell early that morning, adding additional inches to the already snowed-in city.

Aminiature wooden airplane sat on George's bedroom desk. Its lopsided frame tilted in an endless turn. He picked it up and studied the missing parts.

"George?"

Anna was calling his name. He ignored her.

"George?"

Her voice was louder and she was probably standing behind him, but he didn't turn around.

"I'm busy," he said.

"But George."

She must've not heard him. He turned around. Her palm was stretched out to him and she was holding some coins.

"What is it?" he asked.

"I have two dimes, two nickels, and nine pennies," she said. "Can that get Ma to Junior?"

He looked at his sister. She looked worried. "No," he said. "It's not about the money. It's the weather."

"But maybe if we pay them *more*, they'll take her."

"Doesn't work like that," he said. "It keeps snowing and the roads aren't plowed."

Her worried eyes looked at his airplane. He was worried, too. Every evening he heard his mother begging his father to drive her to the Columbus Asylum. But the weather. It wouldn't stop snowing. After New Year's, school was open but only for a day. Since then, they had been snowed in.

"But the mail's getting delivered," she said.

"Yeah, but the mailman's walking."

"But Ma's so worried. And Dad said he can't drive her."

"He can't drive her cuz he has to work," he said. "And he's walking, too. Even if he didn't have to work, there's too much snow right now."

His sister's anxious eyes stared at him.

"But don't worry," he said. "Junior's okay. He's at our state capital. That's where the governor lives."

PAYMENT

State of Ohio
Department of Public Welfare
State Office Building
Columbus 14
January 24, 1951

Name of patient: Walter Janikowski Junior
Addressed To: Walter Janikowski Senior

CONDITIONAL ORDER TO SUPPORT

Under the laws of Ohio, a father, mother,
husband, wife, son, daughter, or guardian of
a patient at the Columbus Asylum is liable
for the support of such patient at the
average per capita cost which at present is
$ 9.80 per week.

Unless you request a modification of the
maximum rate or a release from payment
therefrom within a reasonable length of

time, you are directed to pay the Treasurer
of State $ 9.80 per week, every four weeks,
for the support of the patient.

Frank Olson
Supervisor of Support
Bureau of Support
Division of Mental Hygiene

A line of penciled Xs crossed through the first days of the February 1951 calendar. Anna's finger traced a bold, red circle surrounding the fourth Sunday of the month. The dainty hands of the pretty calendar lady held a soda pop bottle in one hand and a green diary in the other. The red of the lady's lipstick matched the circle around 25th. Anna thought of her mother and Junior, and recalled George's words about the bad weather and driving conditions. She glanced out the front window at the ice coated street and piles of snow, big enough for tunnels.

The mailman stepped into her view. He was heading to the front porch, his body bundled from head to toe and angled against a strong wind. Freezing air blew at her face as she opened the front door.

"Hello, young lady," he said. Puffs of steam floated through his scarf and his eyes were the only part of his face she could see.

"Take this letter to your mother," he said, plopping a cold envelope in her palm.

She looked at the letter. The mailman's gloved fingers clasped her hand.

"Make sure your mother gets it right away," he said.

State of Ohio
Columbus Asylum
Columbus 14, Ohio
February 8, 1951

Re: Walter R. Janikowski #14088

Dear Mrs. Janikowski:

Walter is well and getting along fine. Of
course you realize his limitations and we
can not expect too much of him. However, he
seems to be happy in his new home.

Mr. Jones reports that Walter still drinks
from his bottle some of the time but
gradually he is learning to use a glass. He
must be fed. Mr. Jones has not noticed any
convulsions and none have been reported to
us. You may bring him candy when you visit.
We received the dollar which you enclosed.

Mr. Jones will use this money to buy Walter candy or pop.

There is lettle hope that medicine or surgery will ever be able to help Walter. We feel that he will always need some one to care for him. Be assured that he is getting the best of care.

We will be glad to discuss Walter's case with you anytime you happen to be here on visit. If I happen to be out some one else in the social service department will see you.

Sincerely yours,
Roger S. Gates, M.D.
Superintendent

By: JMHaines
J. M. Haines, Social Worker

NAÏVE OUTLOOK

W alter picked up a piece of stationary on the desk. Ruth's precise handwriting documented details about Junior and questions about his care. It started out as one page, then tripled in just a day. The gap on the calendar narrowed between penciled Xs and a circle of red, and Walter couldn't believe the state of his house. The kitchen pots shined, his clothes were neatly ironed, and when he returned home from work, a hot meal was waiting for him.

She had taken to reading the newspaper, scouring it for any word about the asylum and studying the bus schedule. She discussed how much it would cost for a ticket, but her naïve outlook worried him. He cited numerous bus changes and the unpredictable weather and the hours needed just to arrive at the state capital, let alone find the asylum.

After days of her relentless begging, he gave in and tried to teach her to drive. Despite her fear of machinery and oncoming vehicles, she gripped the steering wheel with shaking hands as she waited for instructions. She nodded her readiness, but he could see her knuckles turning white. He showed her how to put the car in drive and told her to gingerly press the gas pedal. The car lurched forward in the driveway, sliding over ice and skidding into a corner of the house. Shaken, he got out of the car to inspect the damage, only to slip and fall on the icy drive.

"The twenty-fifth is almost here," she said later in the day, marking another X. "I hope the weather is better."

The temperature finally began to warm, but by the time the twenty-fifth arrived, snow and ice from the previous week's weather kept the roadways impassable.

He lifted the February calendar page and peeked at March. Another red circle was there, surrounding the fourth Sunday of the month.

94

ABOVE-NAMED PERSON

St. Dymphna Guild
For Spiritual Welfare of Mentally Deficient
Columbus Asylum
Columbus 14, Ohio
February 26, 1951

In Re: Walter Janikowski Junior

At the Columbus Asylum for the Feeble-
Minded, I am writing to you with the hope
that you will provide further information
regarding the above-named person. Please
fill in the enclosed form completely with
certificates of Baptism, First Holy
Communion and Confirmation to ensure the
spiritual welfare of the patient.

Once a child has sufficient knowledge of his
religious beliefs, he is admitted to the
Sacraments once a month.

To provide the necessities of our chapel, we rely solely upon the charity of our friends. Funds are obtained from your canceled sales tax stamps. We would appreciate your sending as many of these as possible regularly. Will you ask your friends, also, to help this good cause along by their contributions of canceled sales tax stamps.

Assuring you that I will welcome hearing from you at any time relative to this person, I remain,

Sincerely yours,
(Rev) William Harting
per L.L. Marshal

Ruth pulled open a small drawer in the upper half of her desk. She reached for a worn envelope with her handwriting on the front cover and dumped out the contents. Colorful sales tax stamps that she had paper-clipped into groups scattered over her stationary, brightening the dull paper with patterns, letters, and numbers. She looked at the outside of the envelope. Each stamp bunch was earmarked for the church, the nuns, and George and Anna's schools.

She filled out the requested St. Dymphna Guild form, documenting the only achievement Junior met in the church, his baptism. She stared at the charities written on the envelope. Her pencil wavered as she crossed out the nuns.

96

FOREVER DAMAGED

A nna followed her brother into the living room.
"Stop following me," he said.
"I'm not!" she replied. He landed on the sofa and she sat on the floor next to Irene.

"Do you two have your homework done?" her mother asked. She was sitting on the sofa, too, but she was knitting.

"*Mine* is done," Anna said.

"Doin' it now," George replied.

Anna looked at Irene's crayon. It was wiggling and coloring a drawing Anna had made for her earlier that week.

"Why is her hair green?" Anna asked.

Her little sister stopped and looked at the picture.

"Like this," Anna said. She picked up a brown crayon, coloring over the green. She was trying to teach Irene, trying to be patient like her mother, but she wasn't getting it. "And her dress," she said. "The flowers are supposed to be red, not blue." Another mistake.

The telephone rang.

"Want me to get it?" George asked.

She looked at her brother. He would do anything to get out of doing his homework.

"*You* finish your homework, young man." From the sound of her mother's voice, she was thinking the same thing.

The ringing continued until her mother answered the telephone.

Anna handed her sister another sheet of paper. "Here," she said, "you'd better practice."

Suddenly a violent scream erupted from her mother.

Anna turned toward the telephone. Her mother's fingers were rolling open. The receiver dropped to the floor. The telephone stand wobbled as her mother struggled to stand.

Her father raced in from the kitchen grabbing her mother and the telephone. He was frantically yelling into the receiver, asking for an answer.

Anna's heart was forever damaged as she learned her brother was dead.

97

A WARRIOR

An elaborate arrangement of white flowers and green leaves lay on a simple wooden casket. Metal music stands held huge bouquets and filled the warm room as a procession of people dressed in gray and black shuffled by.

Walter approached the casket. The line parted as he neared Junior. A thick layer of makeup covered his son's face, his arms lay crossed over his chest, his stiff fingers curled into fists.

He didn't want to cry, but a teardrop splashed on Junior's suit, darkening the gray to black. He looked at his son. Only a few eyelashes were left. For a moment, he thought he saw them flutter. He touched Junior's sunken cheek, almost expecting him to wake and grunt again. All those embarrassing moments, all those embarrassing grunts, if he could only hear one more, he wouldn't be embarrassed.

"How is your wife doing?"

The question buzzed in his ear. He wasn't sure who was standing next to him. He looked at the first row of folding chairs. Ruth's body was rigid and fixed.

"The best she can," he said, "in a situation like this." What else was there to say? His wife was a warrior. All those battles. All those years. Only to end in the way he knew it would end.

An arm wrapped around his lower back. It was warm and comforting. He turned. It belonged to Ruth's mother.

98

State of Ohio
Department of Health
March 19, 1951

Dear Sir:

This letter will acknowledge your request
for a certified copy of a death certificate
for Walter Janikowski Junior .

The original certificate which you request a
certified copy thereof, will not be
routinely mailed to this office until the
15th day of April 1951 .

Sincerely yours,
(Sgd.) W. R. Robertson, Chief
Division of Vital Statistics

MALNUTRITION

Certificate of Death

Place of Death: Columbus Asylum, Columbus
Ohio
Length of Stay: 2 mos — 9 days
Name of Deceased: Walter Janikowski Junior

Date of Death: March 9, 1951
Date of Birth: March 24, 1934
Age: 16 yrs, 11 mos, 16 days

Medical Certification
Disease or Condition Directly Leading to
Death:
Bronchopneumonia, Bilateral

Antecedent Causes:
Keratitis
Malnutrition
Other Significant Conditions:
Mental Retardation

State of Ohio
Columbus Asylum
Columbus 14, Ohio
March 31, 1951

Dear Mr. & Mrs. Janikowski:

Your letter of March 18 addressed to Dr.
Boray was given to me for reply, inasmuch as
I am the superintendent here. I am very
sorry that you feel the way you do about the
care Walter received here. Although his
physical condition did deteriorate rather
rapidly here, I honestly think it is unfair
to ascribe this to negligence or to lack of
interest in his well-being. Almost all of
the children admitted here do adjust and
actually thrive, but it is true that Walter
did not fall into this group.

As you know, Walter was in the hospital here

for several days prior to his death. He was
being treated for an ulcer on his eye and
had, on the very day of his death, been seen
by our consulting ophthalmologist who did
not see any serious implications in the eye
condition. Late in the afternoon on Friday
March 9, Dr. Traner, the ward physician,
called me at a meeting downtown to report
that Walter had suddenly developed a high
fever, and had gone into shock. I asked that
he notify you folks (which was done) and
employ the usual supportive treatment
measures. This he did and Walter rallied for
a while, only to lapse into unconsciousness
in the early evening. I regret that I was
not here to talk with you myself to explain
that he was seriously ill, but it was my
understanding that such a report had been
made.

The results of the autopsy at the University
Hospital verify the existence of pneumonia
and indicated also that he had a chronic
valvular heart disease plus an internal
hydrocephalus. Convulsions were not observed
in the hospital. The microscopic examination
of the tissues is not available yet; if they
add anything to our understanding of
Walter's illness and the cause of his death,
we shall be glad to notify you.

I can well understand your dissatisfaction
and your feeling of frustration at having
committed Walter here only to have him die
so soon. I sincerely wish that we had been

able to prevent this happening, but I can
only say that I believe that we did the best
we could for him, and I hope that you will
come to believe that too.

Very truly yours,
Roger S. Gates, M. D.
Superintendent

By: JMHaines
J. M. Haines, Social Worker

101

ITEMIZED LIST

State of Ohio
Columbus Asylum
Columbus 14, Ohio
April 6, 1951

Dear Parents:

Enclosed are Walter's clothing that we are
mailing you today.

Slippers, Pants (Woolen), Cotton Shirts,
Drawers, P-Js.

Sincerely yours,
Roger S. Gates, M.D.
Superintendent

By: JMHaines
Social Case Worker

102

OLD OLD STORY

State of Ohio
Department of Public Welfare
Division of Mental Hygiene
April 17, 1951

Dear Mrs. Janikowski:

I have your letter of March 28, in which you
describe the situation relative to your son
who died in the Columbus Asylum. The facts,
as you state them, distress me a great deal
because surely you know that we do not like
for any individual to be neglected in
any way.

As you requested, I have discussed this
situation with the Director and your letter
has been read by him. I am quoting what he
said. "Tell Mrs. Janikowski that you have
discussed the matter with me and that we
will keep in mind what she said when we make

our future plans for the Department." As the
years have gone by, the case load in our
state asylum has increased far out of
proportion to the increase in personnel. As
a result, when we made the change last May
into our present system, we thought we were
being very liberal in adding almost one
hundred employees to the Table of
Organization there. We find now that what we
thought was liberal and an adequate increase
in numbers of individuals is far below what
it should have been. With the addition of
new individuals who do not know the routine
as yet, and still not enough to take up the
entire load, we are faced with the old, old
story of too many patients and not enough
individuals employed who know how to handle
the situation.

I regret very much that this situation has
arisen, and I assure you that had it been in
the power of any of us to prevent it, it
would not have occurred. We can only say
that we will make every effort to prevent
future occurrences, but we are dependent
upon the securing of adequate individuals as
well as adequate dollars to expand the
program so that these unfortunate people can
be adequately cared for in our hospitals.

Sincerely,
William Carter, M.D.
Commissioner
BRR/ e

103

BE GIVEN EVERY CONSIDERATION

State of Ohio
Office of the Governor
Columbus 11
May 8, 1951

Dear Mrs. Janikowski:

Your letter of April 29th to the Governor
relative to your son Walter Janikowski
Junior who recently passed away in the
Columbus Asylum has been referred to me for
acknowledgment.

I have carefully read and noted the content
of your letter.

In order that your letter may be given every
consideration I am forwarding it to Judge
Thompson, Director of Welfare in Ohio, for
his attention.

He will be in contact with you soon.

Very truly yours,
Edward Learner
Secretary to the Governor
LSC/mp

104

THE DETAILS OF YOUR SON'S DEATH

State of Ohio
Department of Public Welfare
State Office Building
Columbus (14)
May 10, 1951

Dear Mrs. Janikowski:

Your letter of April 27th, addressed to the
Governor, has been referred to the
undersigned for attention.

I have directed Dr. Roger S. Gates,
Superintendent of the Columbus Asylum, to
write you immediately and give you a full
report on the death of your son. I feel sure
that if you so desire, he will grant you an
interview and will explain the details of
your son's death to you.

If you do not hear from him within a

reasonable time, please call this matter to
my attention again.

Very truly yours,

J. H. Thompson,
Director of Public Welfare
HLM/c

cc: The Hon.Henry R. Conner
Roger S. Gates, M D

105

EMACIATION

State of Ohio
Columbus Asylum
Columbus 14, Ohio
May 11, 1951

Dear Mr. & Mrs. Janikowski:

Judge J. H. Thompson has called my attention
to your letter addressed to the Governor. I
wrote to you on March 31, describing in some
detail the circumstances surrounding
Walter's death.

I am inclosing a copy of that letter in the
event it failed to reach you.

I have before me here the clinical record
which bears out my belief that Walter had a
thorough admission examination including
physical and psychological studies.

The following is the impression of the examining physician;

Severe mental deficiency (Mental age approximately 13 months on Standard tests although it is likely that his potential was really higher)
Congenital heart disease-cyanotic type; probably a septal defect.
Cerebral palsy; spastic type; involvement most severe in the lower extremities.
Scoliosis

Walter was also seen by the consulting ophthalmologist who found some ocular pathology but ocular treatment was considered inadvisable.

Just yesterday the complete autopsy report arrived from University Hospital. Below is the final diagnosis taken from that report;

Bronchopneumonia
Pulmonary edema
Acute bronchitis
Chronic aortic valvulitis, probably rheumatic in origin
Hydrocephalus, mild, communicating
Cerebral congestion and edema
Emaciation
Mental retardation (clinical)
Marked scoliosis

I list these details to further support the contention that our staff had rather

complete facts about Walter's condition. It
is unfortunate that you did not accompany
Walter when he was admitted so we could have
had the benefit of your understanding of his
special needs.

I should like to emphasize that Walter's
weight loss was not due to the
unavailability of food or lack of interest
in feeding him but rather to an unawareness
of his special needs and his own emotional
reaction to the change in coming here.

We have a whole ward full of children who
require as much care as Walter — who have to
be fed like infants and they do seem to
thrive.

I believe I can understand how you feel and
I do not blame you for being unhappy about
the situation. Perhaps if you would come
down we could sit down and talk about the
problem in its entirety. I should be glad to
show you the complete autopsy report, our
clinical record, and take you to visit some
of the wards so you can see for yourself
that we are successfully caring for a great
many children even more helpless that
Walter.

If after such a visit you still feel that
"this is deliberate murder, brought about by
the superiors at Columbus Asylum" then I
think you should demand a complete
investigation.

Again I reiterate my desire to have the
opportunity to talk to you in person.

Very truly yours
Roger S. Gates, M.D.
Superintendent

By: JMHaines
Social Case Worker

PART VI

1975

Forgotten? No, we never do forget;
We let the years go; wash them clean with tears,
Leave them to bleach out in the open day,
Or lock them careful by, like dead friends' clothes,
Till we shall dare unfold them without pain—
But we forget not, never can forget.
— DINAH MARIA MULOCK CRAIK

106

JIGSAW

Eyeing the cluttered shelves, Walter searched for an oil can in his workshop. He moved random pieces of metal and tarnished jars from the shelves, exposing clean spots beneath each gadget, but he couldn't find the oil can and the search continued. A tape measure that he needed yesterday momentarily distracted him. He pulled at the yellow ruler, exposing two feet. The metal strip quickly rolled back into its home and jostled his mind back to the present. For a moment, he thought he found what he was looking for behind an old jigsaw and food mill, but it was a nut chopper. He tossed the tape measure into an opened cigar box and it clanked into a mixture of nails and broken pencils. A cluster of silver at the bottom of the box caught his attention. His fingers dug through the mottled mixture and hooked onto a ring of keys. Skeleton keys of various lengths and sizes poked out from the ring, like iron paws made of tiny wrenches. The set rested in his opened palm as he studied the vintage keys, wondering where he got them. One of the keys lifted away from the group. His fingers rubbed the stubby end as he marveled at how keys had advanced.

The sound of a car pulling in his driveway startled him. A man's voice was calling his wife's name. He looked out the door. Ruth's white hair shimmered in the sun as the man limped toward her. They were speaking, but he couldn't hear what they were saying. He stepped outside his workshop. He heard the man talking about *Curious George*. And something about hope. Ruth was hugging the man. Was she crying? He wasn't sure. No, they were both smiling.

"I almost forgot!" the man said.

Walter watched as the man hobbled to his car and opened the door. He hovered over the seat, grabbing something from the back. Ruth had her hand on his door, waiting. The man stood up. He was holding a worn, cylindrical can. It still rattled with marbles.

AFTERWORD

Month after month, year after year, decade after decade, I had the same dream. Always the same dream. It was dusk. I was alone in my grandmother's house, standing in her living room. An overwhelming need to close the heavy golden curtains shielding two large picture windows overcame me. Then I would wake.

As a child, I remember hearing snippets of information that my grandmother had another son who died. Questions were never asked and words rarely spoken about this unknown Uncle. One day, I was standing in my grandmother's living room, alone. She entered the room heading to the back of the house. Just inches away, I asked her a question. She stopped, leaned over and quietly said, "Wait right here." I stood in the room alone again, looking out the two huge windows to the world beyond. Uneasiness and anticipation floated through my body, my heart thumped. What was I hoping to know? In a moment, she returned holding a small black and white photograph of a baby. She handed me the image. My fingertips grasped the slim white edge of the weathered photograph, careful not to touch the printed middle. The picture felt cool and glossy between my fingers. A suspended silence threaded the air as I studied the photo of this unusual baby.

About thirty years after my grandmother passed, I inherited her important documents. Among miscellaneous papers and memorial cards, I found letters about her son, responses to some sort of inquiry. The letters were dismissive and arrogant and no real answers ever given. Not only did the mystery deepen, but my grandmother's courage and perseverance became unmistakable.

The events were decades old by the time I was born. It was difficult to believe she experienced such horrific times and yet, there she was. A person filled with kindness and peace and radiating unconditional love. I can't help but marvel at her ability to forgive. Forgive the situation. Forgive other people. And, most importantly, forgive herself.

ACKNOWLEDGMENTS

I would like to acknowledge my lifetime of gratitude to my mother, Mary Whitescarver. Her encouragement, memories, and tears helped make this book possible. A very special thank you to John Kornacki, Barbara Kornacki, Catherine Filiere, Judy Sobzak, Alexandra Bunshaft, Bradley Gayheart, John Whitescarver, Robin Sisak, Denise Russell, Pamela Arendt, and Kelly Urgan.

I would also like to thank Kirsi Hyvaerinen, Ćana Karadžić, Zorka Karadžić, Dragan Karadžić, Anka Karadžić and Gašo Lalović. The hospitality you have sprinkled over me in the beautiful mountains of Montenegro will never be forgotten.

I would like to give credit to the following resources:

Barr, Amelia Edith Huddleston. 1885. "Jan Vedder's Wife."

Barrett Browning, Elizabeth. 1856. "Aurora Leigh."

Chopin, Kate. 1895. "The Kiss." Leicestershire: W.F. Howes Limited, 2014

Craik, Dinah Maria Murlock. 1866. "A Flower of a Day."

De Staël-Holstein, Anne Louise Germaine. 1813. "Germany."

Hemans, Felicia. 1823. "The Siege of Valencia."

Stern, Edith M., *Mental illness: A guide for the family*. New York: the Commonwealth Fund, 1942.

ABOUT THE AUTHOR

Victoria Arendt was born in Toledo, Ohio. Inspired by travel and movement, she has lived in several different locations, including the vibrant city of San Francisco and the rugged mountains of Montenegro. Currently, she lives in Florida with her husband and scruffy dog named Simon. This is her first novel.

Made in the USA
Columbia, SC
28 June 2021

41039738R00195